Dedication

For Agnes, Rita and Peter
Vinny McInerney, Tommy Healey, Bob Pennington

LIVERPOOL SHORT STORY COLLECTION

THE ONE ROAD

A Single Journey ~ Many Lives

JACK BYRNE

Disclaimer:
This is a work of fiction. Names, characters, businesses, places, events, locales, and incidents are either the products of the author's imagination or used in a fictitious manner. Any resemblance to actual persons, living or dead, or actual events is purely coincidental

Introduction

The Liverpool Mystery Series are part family sagas, part historical novels, all thrillers, that cover the period from 1920s Wicklow to Liverpool in 2020. Check out the links at the end for more information.

The four novels are stand-alone thrillers, but in reading all of them, we get more out of each one. The first book I wrote was Under The Bridge. Although it was set in Garston, Liverpool, its roots were in Wicklow, Ireland. The Morning After is the second novel, and it was writing this book that I realised this was a series all along. I am currently writing Fire This Time, and The Wicklow Boys will follow. You can read the novels in any order, and like our lives, they are a moment in time, connected to what happens before and after.

I hope you enjoy this collection of stories; they set the scene and introduce some of the characters and locations from The Liverpool Mystery Series. I am grateful to Northodox Press for cover design, Leila Kirkconnell for advice and reading.

At the time of writing, I am an independent author; the book will sell if you like it, recommend it, and share it on social media.

You can contact me at Jack.byrne.writer@gmail.com

I am always happy to hear people's stories; who knows, your story might be the next one I write.

Enjoy the collection.

Jack Byrne   Twitter @Jackbyrnewriter

Table of Contents

The One Road

It was a horrible start to the day. The wind and rain swirled about outside. Vinny hated darkness in the morning—it seemed unnatural. The gas ring flared up, and the heat from its flame brought a sense of comfort to the dank kitchen. Placing the kettle on the ring, he heard the gas hissing as it was forced through the nozzles and the quiet roar as the heat broke the equilibrium of the water inside. The kettle was home to a storm of its own.

He took his tea into the living room and balanced it on the arm of the settee while he rolled a ciggy. The actions came easily. Years of student life had taught his hands to roll instinctively. He lit the ciggy and sat back with eyes closed. As the smoke filled his lungs, he felt the calming effect of nicotine.

The phone rang, its harsh tone breaking through his relaxation. He jumped, knocking both his tea and the ashtray off the arm of his chair.

"Shit."

The cup bounced on the floor, spilling its contents over the carpet, leaving a brown steaming stain. The ashtray rolled across the floor with a trail of cigarette stumps in its wake.

"Bastard."

The phone was still ringing. "Okay, I'm coming."

He picked up the receiver. "Hello?"

"Morning, Mr Connolly, this is your alarm call." Vinny

recognised Kevin's voice immediately.

"And fuck you too." He spat back into the phone.

"See, you had a good night, then?"

"What are you ringing for?"

"To make sure you're awake. What do you think? To hear your pleasant voice?"

"Okay, so now I'm awake."

"Well, get your arse round here then."

"Okay, okay. I'm on my way." Vinny said.

As he stepped outside, a gust of rain-filled wind hit him in the face. He put his head down and raced across the street to the van, which had seen better days. The asbestos campaign had bought it second hand from a community kids' group. Years of running around full of screaming children had taken its toll. It looked like a refugee from the war in Bosnia: its once royal blue paintwork was now battered and scratched. One wing mirror was held in place by black insulation tape, and its headlights strayed in different directions like a bog-eyed monster.

He pulled the choke out full before turning the ignition. It took four attempts of guttural churning before the engine caught in a whine. A freezing draught was blowing in through the side window, which didn't close properly. He turned the heater on full even though he knew it would be blowing out cold air until the engine warmed up.

Daylight was beginning to break, exposing the dark clouds to sight. It was getting on for 7 am, and Vinny was due in Speke at 7:45 am.

***

He turned off Lark Lane into a broad street of tall houses, Victorian homes of merchants now divided into cramped bedsits. He pulled up outside Kevin's, and looking up to the first floor, he could see the light was on.

Minutes later, Kevin was in the street.

"Alright?"

"Will be when I wake up." Kevin slammed the van door behind him.

"Hey, take it easy on the old girl." Vinny had kept the engine running, and a stale-smelling warm air wafted through the cab.

"Right, we're off then." Vinny put the van into gear, and it lurched forward.

"Whose funeral is it anyway," asked Kevin.

"It's one of the old guys who was in the group."

Vinny turned the radio on to drown out the flapping of the windscreen wipers. He liked music when he was driving, even at this time in the morning.

"God, I hope this weather clears up." Vinny reached forward to wipe the condensation from the windscreen.

"How come we're going to Wales?" Kevin asked.

"Because that's where his family is from."

"Well, what was he doing in Liverpool?"

"I don't bleeding know. I only met him once."

Kevin feigned outrage. "Well, that's very nice, isn't it. Can't you show some respect? You're supposed to be campaigning for these people."

"Well, there's not much campaigning can do for the old bastard now, is there?"

"That's a terrible, terrible attitude to have." The outrage was less feigned this time.

"Will you shut up. It's seven in the morning, pissing down, and I've got to drive a bunch of plebs to a funeral in taffy land. I don't need you on my case. Now, give me a break."

Kevin turned and stared out of the window as Vinny drove them in silence through Allerton toward Speke. He'd followed the route for the airport but was now heading toward the estate. He knew the area like the back of his hand. He had grown up, and his past was still there. His mum and an ex-girlfriend both lived a few streets away. Unlike the rest of the estate, which was built just after the Second World War, Dymchurch had been built in the previous five years. The road curved round the older houses, with cul-de-sacs branching off it in every direction. Planners had inadvertently created a haven for car thieves or anyone else trying to outrun the police.

Keeping to Dymchurch Road, they soon found seventy-two. The rain had subsided, and though still blustery, the night had given way to a sharp early light. Vinny turned off the engine.

"Right. What I know is the guy had asbestosis, his wife and kids live in Wales, and he is getting buried there this afternoon. All we have been asked to do is to take some of his family over to the funeral."

"Okay, gotcha, but what's the deal with the University?"

"There isn't one, really. A professor suggested that I would be doing myself a favour if I joined the asbestos campaign group. It's called social research. To be honest, I would've joined a fucking necrophilia group if kept me on the course. Right...are you ready?"

Kev nodded. "Come on, let's get on with it."

The door was opened by a boy of around ten who ran straight back into the house, leaving them standing on the doorstep. They could hear him inside. "Nan, der's a black man at the door."

Kevin shrugged. "Fuckin hillbillies."

A minute later, a slight, grey-haired woman appeared at the door. She was wearing dark grey trousers and a black jumper and cardigan.

Vinny was the first to speak. "Hello, I'm Vincent Connolly, and this is Kevin Lucas. We're here to take you to Wales."

"Oh, yes, of course. Come in." She held the door open and led them through the hall to the living room.

The boy who had opened the door had already forgotten their existence and sat in front of the TV.

"I'm Renee, and this is Ian. Say hello, Ian." She tried to divert his attention from the television.

His head turned slightly while his eyes remained fixed on his programme. The only sound he produced was a "Right" that came out of the side of his mouth.

"It's Mrs Doyle, isn't it?" asked Vinny.

"Not now. It's Morgan. Renee Morgan. You can call me Renie. Doyle was my maiden name. Jack was my brother. His family are in Anglesey, though he was staying with us when he died. He was on the ships, you see, so he spent a lot of time in Liverpool. Not that he's worked for a long time, what with the illness and everything. He was over here seeing some of his friends, sort of saying goodbye, you might say, when it happened. But I'm forgetting my manners, would you like a cup of tea before we set out?

"I'd love one, thanks," said Kevin.

"Yeah, me too. Thanks," Vinny added.

"Well, if you'll excuse me, I'll go and sort it out."

Mrs Doyle or Morgan was in her sixties. Though not big, she had an energy and life that belied her age. She returned a minute later with two steaming mugs of tea on a tray with a bowl of sugar.

"Help yourselves," she said, placing the tray on a small coffee table in front of them and disappearing again into the kitchen.

Vinny took a drink of the tea. The loss of his tea earlier had left his throat parched. This was just the trick.

A female voice rang out. "Mam, have you ironed my black dress?"

The door from the hallway was thrown open, and a young woman with her head wrapped in a towel walked in, wearing only her knickers and bra. She was drying her hair vigorously, causing her small breasts to jiggle about. She stood in the centre of the room, just feet in front of the coffee table. Kevin couldn't take his eyes off the slim but shapely legs that led to a perfectly shaped bum, covered by the thinnest pair of knickers he'd seen in some time.

Kevin coughed loudly. "Ahhemmm"

The figure in front of them froze before lifting the towel

slowly. Kevin waved at the pretty face that peeked out from under.

"Aaaarrrhh." There was an ear-piercing scream as she scrambled for the door, knocking over the coffee table in the process. Vinny's tea went flying for the second time that morning.

"Hey, things are looking up," Kevin said, smiling as he righted the coffee table and put his mug back on it.

Mrs Morgan rushed back into the room. "What happened?"

Without turning from the television, Ian saved them from embarrassment. "It was our Susan. She knocked his tea over."

Renie went to get a cloth to wipe the table and scrub the carpet.

"Ian, turn that telly off and go and get your coat on," she said as she returned to scrub the steaming spot on the carpet.

It reminded Vinny that his own carpet would be stained by now.

"Mrs Morgan...sorry, Renie...how many people are we taking?" Vinny asked.

"Well, there's me, Ian, Susan, and then the lads." She took the cloth out to the kitchen, clipping Ian round the head as she passed. "I told you to get your coat on."

Ian jumped up and ran behind the sofa. He returned, putting his arms through a black nylon jacket with the LA Raiders logo on the back, and sat back down in front of the television. Renie came through from the kitchen, wearing a knee-length overcoat and carrying a black handbag. She turned the TV off and pulled Ian to his feet. "Go and tell your sister to get a move on."

When Ian left the room, Renie opened her handbag and handed Vinny a photograph. "Jack's the one in the middle."

Renie went into the hallway and called out, "Susan, we're waiting for you. Now get a move on."

Kevin leaned across to look at the photo. A group of young men stood on the deck of a ship, a funnel clearly visible behind them. Kevin thought the man at the centre of the group would be able to handle himself. His tight-fitting t-shirt covered a well-contoured body. A bull neck carried a sharply featured face.

"Jeez, wouldn't fancy meeting him in a dark alley," Kevin whispered.

"I'm not surprised. He's the one that's dead, you dickhead."

Popping her head round the door, Renie called in, "Right, we're ready."

"What about the lads you mentioned?" asked Vinny.

"We'll pick them up on the way," Renie replied.

"Okay, let's move."

Susan was hiding behind her mum, Renie, and avoiding eye contact with anyone.

Kevin greeted her with a "Good morning, Susan."

She blushed but didn't respond. Instead, she opened the front door and led them down the path to the van. The rain had stopped, but a buffeting wind stung the skin, and they stood, shivering until Kevin opened the back doors. "Okay, everyone in. Susan, do you want to sit up front, show us where to pick up the others?"

"I will! I know where it is," Ian shouted as he raced round to the passenger door.

Renie and Susan climbed in the back and sat on the bench-like seats that ran the length of the van.

"Are you okay back there?" Vinny asked over his shoulder.

"It's freezing," Susan complained.

"That'll teach you to put some proper clothes on in future," Renie snapped.

"It'll warm up when we get going." Vinny turned the ignition and was surprised to hear the engine kick into life the first time.

"It's that way." Ian pointed out the window.

It was 8.15 am on a Saturday morning, and the estate had a desolate feel to it. The wind picked up and carried litter and leaves over the grass verges and along the gutters. Twenty-five thousand people lived on the estate. Yet, the streets were empty. Vinny was glad he didn't live here anymore.

"It's straight-up till you get to The Parade." Sitting in the front, Ian was delighting in his newfound position of authority. The dual carriageway they had been driving along ended abruptly. The road swung round to the left.

"That's the Parade." Ian pointed as they passed a square of multi-coloured steel-shuttered shops.

The shutters were provided by the local council in an attempt to attract and secure traders, and at the same time to dissuade local thieves. The shutters brought a false sense of energy and life to the run-down shops.

"Here, turn now. Here, you can go in the car park."

"The Noah's, " Vinny announced unnecessarily.

"The Noah's Ark," Ian confirmed.

"It's eight o'clock on a Saturday morning; what are we stopping at a pub for?" Vinny asked.

"We won't be long," Renie called out from the back. "Ian, go and get your dad."

She fished in her handbag for her cigarettes. She offered one to Susan. "The lads have been saying goodbye to Jack. Do you want one?" She offered the pack to Kevin and Vinny.

"No, thanks," said Vinny.

"Yeah, I will." Kevin leaned over the front seat.

"Here, pass this to the front." Renie handed a cigarette to Susan.

For the first time since they were in the house, Susan let her eyes meet with Kevin's.

He smiled and said, "Thanks," though casual, it still carried his interest, an interest not completely unnoticed or unwelcomed by Susan.

Vinny turned the radio on and, covered by its sound, asked Kevin, "What the fuck are they doing in the pub?"

"I think we are about to find out," Kevin replied.

Ian jumped out and ran to the pub doors. They couldn't see inside the pub since all the curtains were drawn. He started banging on the graffiti-covered steel doors. They heard the screech of bolts being pulled back, and the door opened just enough to let Ian disappear into the darkness beyond before slamming shut.

They waited in silence. The radio provided the only distraction as its melodies filled the cold van. The pub doors were finally thrown open, and Ian ran to the front of the van.

"In the back." Vinny pointed with his thumb.

"Oh, come on, I showed you how to get here," Ian pleaded.

"Ian!" The single word from Renie sent him scuttling round to the back, out of sight and earshot of his grandmother, but not before he spat at Vinny, "Ye Meth."

The pub entrance was suddenly full of staggering and swaying figures, arms clasped around each other, whether in friendship or physical support, it was unclear.

"How many are we taking?" Vinny asked nervously.

"Don't panic, just a couple." Renie volunteered from the back. "There's our John now," she added.

A tall, well-built figure detached himself from the group and made his way over to Vinny's side of the van. He tapped on the window. Vinny wound it down.

"Alright, mate." A strong hand was thrust through quickly, followed by the smell of stale alcohol.

Vinny shook the proffered hand. "Are you ready to go?"

"Will be, just give us a minute."

The rest of the group, about six in all, made their way to the van. Vinny noticed a scruffy old mongrel hanging about at the edge of the group.

John opened the back doors. "Come on, Liam, get in."

After much backslapping, handshaking, and best wishes, Liam climbed in the back. The dog jumped in after them.

Vinny turned round. "Get that thing out. Come on, we

should get going."

"That's Sandy," said Ian. "He goes everywhere with our Liam."

"Well, I'm sorry, but he's not coming with us," Vinny said.

John left his seat in the back and moved forward until he was right behind Vinny. "The dog's coming," he said in a low clear voice.

Vinny turned and looked directly at John, who repeated, "Vincent, the dog is coming."

The look on John's face left no room for doubt.

"I think we'd better take the dog," Kevin advised.

"Okay, the fucking dog can come," Vinny conceded.

"Mind your language," John warned. "There are women here."

"Yeah, ye puff," Ian chimed in before getting a clip round the head from John.

"And that's enough from you as well."

"Right, are we ready to move?" Vinny asked.

"Oh, my God, you've left Jack!" Renie exclaimed.

"Shit, c'mon Liam, give me a hand," John said.

They jumped out of the van, and followed by the men outside the pub, disappeared back inside. When they came out, they were carrying a coffin between them.

"Imagine forgetting Jack," declared Renie.

Vinny was mumbling to himself, "I don't believe this. I just don't believe it."

Kevin pulled the handle on his door. "You said we were taking the relatives, not the stiff. I'm not going. These people are crazy."

Vinny leaned across to pull the door closed again. "The last thing I need is you pulling a moody, so sit there and shut up."

Kevin leaned over to Vinny. "Call me strange, but I don't travel with dead things. You might, these fucking hillbillies might, but I don't travel with things that are dead!"

The back doors of the van were opened, and although he refused to turn round and look, Vinny could hear the scraping of the coffin as it slid over the metal floor into the van.

"Susan, will you move your feet and let Jack in," John said above the grunts and groans and the wood on metal screeching as they struggled to get the coffin in the van.

"Mam, do I have to?" Susan appealed to her grandmother.

Renie called out, "Yes, you do…Why don't you go up front? Vincent, would that be okay with you if our Susan sits up front?"

"Yeah, that's fine," Kevin shouted back.

Vinny turned to Kevin. "I thought you weren't coming?"

"Well, I can't leave you here on your own. Can I?" Kevin said, opening the door and shifting over to make room for Susan.

Susan accepted Kevin's offered hand as she climbed into the front. "Thanks. I don't think I could have stood it back there."

"No problem," Kevin replied as his eyes strayed to a flash of nylon-covered thigh when Susan adjusted her dress.

"Here, let me fix your seatbelt," he offered.

"No, thanks, I can manage," she replied.

"Is everyone in now?" Vinny asked, turning around.

He could hardly see the coffin, not just because people sat in the back had to rest their feet on its polished surface, but the end near the back door was covered in beer cans. Sandy, the dog, Ian, and his father John were on one side while Renie and the old man Liam were sat across the coffin from them.

Liam had known Jack for over fifty years. Brought up in Wicklow, they had lived in Strand Street on The Murrough, a thin strip of land with the River Varty on one side and the Irish Sea on the other. Post-war England needed men for construction, and so they set out on their journey together. They talked their way onto a ship from Arklow, loaded with timber. Their task was to help at the Garston end, mainly cleaning, sweeping out the deck and hold, after the dockers had unloaded. Liam went on to London, lured by a cousin with promises of work in building trade, but he was soon back 'under the bridge' with money in his pocket and looking to settle. Jack decided to stay local to Garston docks until his travels with the 'Merch' opened the world for him.

Jack found his first jobs in the pubs on King Street. If you were young and fit enough, an uncle, brother, or cousin would make the introductions, and in the next few days, he walked down King Street with a kitbag slung over his shoulder—a walk of 500 yards that ended in the brothels and bars of Lagos, Cape Town, and Sierra Leone.

Except for the war years, the Merchant Navy was a good life. Contrasting weeks or months of boredom and hard work in engine rooms or sea whipped decks with the rush of weekends in far-flung ports. Prostitutes and tricksters of every kind queued to divest the unwary sailor of his months of hard-earned and jealously guarded wages.

The war years were different. Tens of thousands of seamen were killed. There were no fanfares, parades, or welcome home for these men, many of whom never survived the North Atlantic convoys or the freezing Baltic. Irishmen, whose lives were used in the service of Britain's war aims, were spat at and called cowards for not wearing a uniform when walking the streets of home ports. Chinese seamen abused and ridiculed as 'Chinks' but recruited in thousands during the war, were rounded up and deported from Liverpool in early morning raids after the war was won. Families and children were robbed of fathers who had risked their lives on British ships.

Liam heard that Jack was ill and knew he had been living somewhere in Wales. In the end, Jack couldn't walk without gasping for breath. The fabric of his lungs had been eaten away by Mesothelioma, lung cancer caused by breathing in asbestos fibres. If he had the foresight to photograph all the engine and boiler-room pipes lagged in asbestos that he worked on over the years, then maybe at the end of his life, he would have been able to claim compensation, but without 'evidence' what could anyone do except watch a vigorous and energetic man turn slowly into a thin and fragile old man, an old sailor who could see his ship sailing out of port on its final voyage.

"Okay, we're off!" Vinny put the van in gear, and to the cheers and claps of the remaining well-wishers outside the pub, they were on their way. "Right, well, I know we're going to Anglesey, but does anyone know where in Anglesey?"

"Hang on a minute, I've got an address." Renie searched through her bag, eventually producing a dog-eared envelope. "Here we are, Our Lady of the Sea and St. Winefride Church, Amlwch, Anglesey."

"Okay, I'm sure we will find it when we get there," Vinny said, adding, "Remember Kev, you're supposed to be navigating for me."

"No problem," Kevin replied, unfolding a map.

Vinny drove out of Speke and on to the Ford Road. He turned the radio back on and relaxed into driving, relieved to be finally on the road and getting some miles on the clock.

"Would the driver like a drink?" John had passed forward a half-full lemonade bottle. Kevin turned to accept the bottle and passed it on to Vinny.

"Open it for me?" Vinny asked.

After it was passed to him, keeping one hand on the wheel, he raised the bottle to his lips. It was only after his first large gulp, and when he was into his second, the potency of the liquid hit his parched throat. His body sprang forward in reaction, pulling his arm down, sending the van swerving wildly to the right, which prompted a crescendo of horn blowing from surrounding traffic. He couldn't stop the second gulp but managed to spit out the remaining vodka from his mouth.

John called out from the back, "Steady on, driver, we only want to bury Jack today!"

"I thought it was lemonade," Vinny protested to Kevin.

Kevin took the bottle, raised it to his mouth, had a drink, and passed it back to John "Vodka...Nice one."

The van rumbled over the Runcorn Bridge. Way below, the Mersey wound its way through to Lancashire, silted up in between mud banks a narrow channel of water, flashing grey in the morning sunlight. Over the bridge, they were in Cheshire and heading for North Wales.

"So, these are all your family?" Kevin asked Susan.

"Liam was Jack's friend, but yeah, Renie's me nan, John's me dad, Ian's me brother, and Jack was me nan's brother." The names and relationships rolled off her tongue.

"And who's brother is the dog?" Kevin asked.

"Very funny," Susan said, turning away from him.

Kevin kicked himself, not only for pushing Susan away but for ridiculing what he envied. Susan's messy family was just that, a family.

John and Liam had spent the night in the Noah's Ark, grabbing snatches of sleep, waking up to songs and more drinks, a combination of exhaustion and intoxication had left them in a strange mood of elation. Still drinking from a can of lager, John was giving a rendition of Danny Boy.

"C'mon, Liam, gives us a song, one of the old ones," Renie asked. "Let Liam have a go."

John relented. "Hey driver, turn the radio off. Show some respect. Liam's gonna give us a song."

"God, this is embarrassing." Susan stared pointedly out of the side window.

"Dad, I'll sing. I've got a song. Go'ed, dad, let me sing." Ian tugged at his father's shirt.

"No, it's Liam's turn. C'mon, Liam."

Ian refused to be ignored and, in tune with the popular football chant, began, "Oh lay, Oh lay -Oh lay, Oh lay."

Then in rhyme, he finished with "Su-san's got no knickers-on today."

"Dad, will you stop him?" Susan's appeal to her father was acted on immediately as he turned and smacked Ian round the head. It was a light slap but enough to sting Ian's pride if not his head, and he sulked back along the side of the van.

"It's not fair. You never let me do anything," Ian complained.

"Ian, come and sit over here, near me," Renie said, trying to console him.

"No, I'm staying here," he answered.

"Okay, if you want a song, this one's for Jack," Liam declared.

Liam straightened himself up and cleared his throat with a few coughs, shifting the mucus lining in his lungs so that his cough turned into a deep chesty convulsion, which was only subdued by spitting its product into a hankie and taking a drink of lager.

"Right, here we go then." The deeply scarred voice kept the rhythm of a marching song.

"We're on the one road, sharing the one load.

We're on the road to God knows where."

"Well, he got that bit right," Kevin interrupted from the front.

"We're on the long road, maybe the wrong road, But we're together now; who cares."

Vinny was listening, amazed at how appropriate the lyrics were.

"Northmen, Southmen, Comrades all, Dublin, Belfast, Cork, and Donegal,

We're on the one road, swinging along, Singing the soldier's song."

Kevin gave Vinny a nudge. "This is a bit heavy, isn't it. Isn't this an IRA song?"

"I'm not sure, but if I were you, I'd keep your mouth shut," Vinny replied.

John spoke first from the back. "Come on, Liam, can't you pick something else. We don't want to bring politics into this."

"You asked me for a song, and I gave you one. If you don't like it, that's your problem."

"Well, it's a bit hard. All I wanted was a sing-along, and you give us all this about the IRA."

"I like it," said Ian, breaking out into his version of the chorus.

"On a long road, on the wrong road singing the soldier's song."

"Ian, stop that," Renie snapped.

"What's that smell?" Vinny was lowering the window.

"Jeez," Kevin added.

"No, blaspheming, if you don't mind," rebuked Renie.

"Sorry, Mrs Morgan," Kevin apologised.

"Dad," Susan shouted, wrinkling her nose.

"Ian." John turned toward Ian.

Ian's hand shot up, expecting to deflect the coming

blow. "It was Sandy!" he exclaimed.

John's hand stopped in mid-air. "That dog's disgusting."

"Okay, that's it. I'm pulling in," Vinny called out.

"Hurry up, then." Kevin urged.

Susan had her head out of the window.

"Come on, pull up," John shouted.

"I can't. You'll have to wait till we get to a lay-by." Vinny pulled over to the nearside lane. "Right, here we go."

Before the van had come to a stop, both the side door and the back doors were open. As it skidded to a halt, the van emptied in seconds.

"Okay, let's take a break, stretch your legs. Can someone see if that dog needs to empty its bowels?" Vinny asked.

"Ian," Renie called, "Sort Sandy out, will you."

Leaning against the van and lighting a cigarette, Kevin spoke quietly. "These lot are crazy."

"They're not that bad. If we keep up a steady speed, it all be over by this afternoon."

"We've got a stiff, a bunch of hillbilly terrorists and a farting dog in the back, and you think it's okay?"

"I haven't heard you complain about Susan." Vinny smiled.

"Yeah, well, they can't be all mad, can they?"

Ian came back with Sandy.

"Right, come on, guys." Vinny led the way.

Everyone was back in and settled.

"Time to get some miles in now. No stopping for at least another hour."

"Even if Sandy strikes again?" laughed Ian.

"Then the dog can drive you there because I'm not." Vinny steered the van smoothly back into the flow of traffic.

If Vinny knew what was coming, he would have turned round and headed back to Liverpool.

***

Kevin was acutely aware of Susan's proximity, or to be more precise, the proximity of her body. He struggled to dismiss the images of Susan in her underwear. In the absence of conversation or distraction, it was difficult. He tried to keep his eyes on the road and off the slim, graceful legs in black tights that were visible beneath her black dress.

The van was rolling along through the Cheshire countryside. The mid-morning sun was climbing in the sky, and the early chill had disappeared. Everyone had settled down and rolled with the van. Susan was looking out of the window. The van swerved sharply.

"Whooaah," Vinny exclaimed. "Bloody potholes."

The sharp turn had thrown Kevin into Susan. He shifted back in the seat and turned his head toward her. Their eyes met. She smiled, and his pulse increased in response. *God, she's pretty.* He relaxed into the seat and allowed his shoulder to rest against Susan. As the van moved on, they were both conscious of the physical connection they shared. It was exciting for Kevin.

***

Liam yawned. It had been a long night. The snatches of sleep between the songs of the night before were not enough for a man of his age. Tiredness was not the only thing bothering him. Beneath his feet was a man he had known for over fifty years. He raised a foot and looked at the coffin beneath. He wouldn't have minded a few scrapes—he'd had enough in life.

What does John know? 'Don't bring politics into it.' As if we had any choice. The Brits control and divide our country, but we are bringing politics into it if we sing a song. Liam could still remember the indignation he felt when he was called Mick for the first time in insult.

There had always been a bit of banter between the men on the site. They were from all over the UK and Ireland. Yet there was something about the way the foreman called him a 'Mick' that had nothing to do with banter. The foreman, a stocky man from London, could and did make Liam feel like nothing, a nobody, like shit on his shoe. If there was a dirty or difficult job, the foreman would laugh and say, "Don't worry, I'll get the Mick to do it."

Liam didn't last long in that job, not after breaking the foreman's nose. He still chuckled at the memory. About five men were sitting in a half-finished office building having their break and a cup of tea. The foreman must have had a bad morning because he had already sacked one bloke. He came up to the group and began cursing about lazy workers and shitty materials. One of the Geordie co-workers told him to chill out. His response was to threaten to sack all of them on the spot for taking too long over their break. As they packed up their gear to get to back to work, the Geordie said, "He needs a fucking slap to shut up him up." Liam stood up and said, "Don't worry, the Mick'll do it." And to the cheers of the others, he did as he promised.

Not everything was so easy to deal with. He didn't support the IRA, but then again, he was from Wicklow, not the north, where 15,000 British troops patrolled the streets. He had never actually seen the famous 'no blacks - no Irish' signs, but it didn't take long to realise he was valued only as a source of labour or revenue.

Labour on the building sites; the motorways were the big ones. If you got on one of those, you would have work for as long as you wanted. But there were rebuilding jobs all over the country after the war, and young Irish men had the skills to fill them: strong bodies and low costs. Liam and tens of thousands like him were a source of income as they moved from place to place—itinerants staying in digs and shared rooms. Work and the pub, the digs for crashing, unheated shared rooms were no fun. You got your job in the pub, warded off the loneliness and cold in the pub, and got paid in the pub. His old friend in the coffin had done well: met and married a Welsh girl, went off to the country to live a quiet life. Jack worked on the coasters, moving coal, timber, copper from port to port around the UK. There was a steady flow from Wales to Liverpool. These short hops meant Jack could have a reasonable family life as a seaman.

"Are you sure they're all alive back there?" Kevin asked. "It's very quiet."

"I hope at least one of them is dead, or it's wasted journey." Vinny joked.

"I'm glad we're amusing to you," Susan threw back at him. She leaned over and turned the radio on. As she did so, she let her foreman rest on Kevin's knee. When she found a station she liked, she straightened up, leaving her left leg resting alongside his. Kevin could feel the warmth of her flesh through the denim of his jeans. He turned his head as if to look out of the side window. Susan was smiling at him.

"Sorry to wake everyone up, but I could do with a cup of tea. A services is coming up. Who's for stopping?" Vinny asked over his shoulder.

Renie added her support. "A cup of tea would be lovely."

The rhythm of the van and the effects of the previous night had taken their toll. Liam and John were asleep.

At Vinny's announcement of the impending stop, Susan moved her leg away from Kevin's.

"Can someone wake that lot up?" Vinny asked.

Kevin obliged by reaching out and turning the radio up full blast. The pounding screech of Motorhead vocals was matched by Sandy, who began to howl in recognition of a kindred spirit in the heavy metal vocalist.

"For Christ sakes…"

The screams, both canine and human, bounced off the metal sides of the van. Renie held her head in her hands. Ian stood on the coffin playing his best air guitar. The sleepers were dragged into wakefulness by what seemed a sound from the very depths of hell. Fortunately, Vinny, Susan, Ian, and Kevin were all out of the van and on their way into the Little Chef before the men could aim blows.

Ian led the way. Susan was closely followed by Kevin while Renie lingered behind, chatting to Vinny. It wasn't the black overcoat or handbag on what turned out to be a bright autumnal morning that looked out of place to Vinny. It was the control this woman had, a composure that lived in the creases of her worn face. There was a bearing of dignity despite the loose threads dangling from her hem. Her face and voice were inseparable, each relying on the other for full impact. It was as he was speaking to her that Vinny realised faces aren't lived in—they are constructed, sculpted by years of careful artistry.

"I haven't had a chance to thank you yet," Renie opened.

"Oh, no problem." Vinny batted away the thanks and then added, "Although, to be honest, I didn't realise we'd be taking the coffin."

"I know. Sorry about that, but we couldn't afford an undertaker to take him all the way Wales in a hearse."

"Sick isn't it: even when you've gone, they are still queuing up with their hand out."

The others were entering the service station. Renie reached out and closed Vinny's hand around a twenty-pound note.

"No, there's no need for that." He offered the money back.

"Don't be daft. You've saved us a fortune."

"No, look, you can't afford this."

They were about to enter the restaurant when Renie stopped him. "Take it. Don't pretend you don't need it." She looked him in the eye and added, "And don't tell me what I can or can't afford."

Vinny knew there was no point in arguing. "Thanks."

Kevin, Susan, and Ian were sat in a semi-circular booth. Vinny and Renie joined them.

"I ordered a large pot of tea," Kevin announced, looking pleased with himself.

"Okay, good." There was enough room for Vinny and Renie to join them around the table.

Vinny began to pour from the pot.

John and Liam entered with Sandy trailing behind on his lead.

"Did you get us a tea?" John asked.

"No, I didn't," Renie replied. "If you want to stay out all night drinking, don't expect me to run around after you."

"Excuse me, sir." A youth in the standard red and white uniform of Little Chef was standing behind Joe.

"Dad, he's talking to you," Ian announced.

"Sir, I'm afraid we don't allow dogs in the restaurant."

John turned and took a step closer to the youth, who took a step backwards. "Well, excuse me. Why are you telling me? Do you think I would keep a mangy old mutt like that?"

"I'm sorry, sir. I thought you were the head of the party."

"He is head of the party every night in the Noah's, leaving me to look after these two." Renie nodded toward Ian and Susan.

"Nan…" Susan complained.

"Don't you start 'Nanning me.' Fix your clothes—

you're showing everything you've got."

Susan, embarrassed, adjusted her dress.

"She's got nothing to show," Ian declared. "I've seen her in the bath."

"If you want a crack, you're going the right way to get one," Renie shot at Ian.

John, pleased by being recognised as 'head of the party,' leaned into the youth and half-whispered,

"That's okay, son, you leave it to me."

"Thank you, sir."

"Liam, will you get the mutt out of here," John asked.

"I haven't had my tea yet," he objected.

Susan volunteered. "Here, I'll take him out."

Kevin made a great show of finishing his tea. "Yeah, I think I could do with some air as well."

"What a surprise," Renie muttered.

Once outside, Susan led the way. Each step crunching on the graveled car park.

"You didn't have to come out you know." The sharp words and a steely looked were flung at Kevin.

"Yeah, I know I didn't." He decided to go for it. "And I don't have to like you either, but I do."

"You don't even know me," she replied, trying to hide her pleasure.

Kevin caught up with her. "Well, maybe if I can get to know you?" He held her arm, and she came to a stop. They stood facing each other, and the dog came to a rest at Susan's feet.

"Come on, what do you say?" he appealed.

A flicker of a smile flashed across her face, and sensing his proximity to success, Kevin reached down for her hand. She let her fingers form around his, and he leaned forward to kiss her.

"Shit."

Kevin pulled back, shocked. "What's wrong? I thought you liked me?"

"Not that, you idiot, the van. Where's the van?"

Kevin looked round. "What's up with you? It's parked over there." As he looked around, he realised that where the van was parked only minutes before, there was now space. "Oh shit. Vinny's not going to like this."

"Never mind Vinny, what about me Nan?"

***

RRRHHHMMM....RRRHHHMMM....RRRHHHMMM....

The noise and vibrations of the constant traffic were fighting their way into his consciousness. Jez raised his head, shaking his dreadlocked hair and rubbing his eyes. His brain struggled to engage his body. His eyes refused to focus. His head wouldn't stay upright but kept flopping first to one side and then the other. His ears were bombarded with the sound of furious engines propelling the vividly coloured shapes that flashed by, which his brain assumed to be cars.

"AAARRRGGHHH"

Giving up the struggle to raise himself, he sank back, his head resting on the ground and his nose twitching with the smell of the soft, damp grass. He closed his eyes to shut out the cruel blue sky. He wished for darkness and enough noise to drown out the sound of the cars. *Fucking daylight.* He hated daylight, especially after a good night. In fact, he hated it after a bad night too. He hated it after any night.

For half an hour, his need for nicotine fought his denial of the new day, and nicotine eventually won out as it did every day. Slowly but surely, he struggled to sit up after the first two attempts were failures. From a distance, he could be mistaken for a yoga practitioner as his head and legs were raised repeatedly while his backside and body remained glued to the ground. He rolled over onto his stomach, and from this position, the task could be achieved with much less energy. Once sitting, he gave a grunt of satisfaction. Now for the search.

The problem with combat jackets was the number of pockets, each containing the paraphernalia of poverty, half-smoked dog ends, an empty matchbox, a half-eaten packet of Polo, some loose matches, a three-inch bookmaker's biro. He wondered where the bookmaker's biro came from as he didn't bet. He didn't support the exploitation of horses in racing. Finally, he found a crumpled packet of Golden Virginia with Rizla papers.

While his fingers expertly and automatically rolled a ciggie, he kicked Dog, who was lying next to him. "Hey, Dog."

If Jez had a best mate, it would be Dog. He didn't have a best mate because he considered himself a lone spirit. So, he had Dog. They met six months earlier when Jez had been on the road with the Astral tribe, a loose collective of nomadic spirits who sought an alternative lifestyle to the growing automation and commercialisation of modern life. The tribe had been passing through Warwickshire when Dog appeared. No one remembered his arrival, and no one remembered his departure when he left with Jez. This was not surprising in the fluctuating world of a travelling community, especially when everything about Dog except his appearance was totally unremarkable. Even his cropped orange hair and nose rings were commonplace in the tribe.

Dog was younger than Jez and latched onto him. Jez didn't know his real name, but his tribal name was Squatting Dog. This name was won after he defecated in front of a farmer who was trying to evict them from his land. In the six months they had been together, Dog had become more than a little attached to Jez. In fact, he idolised him. He followed him through many a skirmish with police as they tied, chained, and glued themselves to various bits of industrial equipment in an attempt to slow down the destruction of Britain's wild environment.

Environmental protection had traversed the landscape of politics from being the preserve of people like Jez, who had climbed up trees and dug down tunnels, to the boardrooms and committees of private companies and N.G.O.'s. Time and the movement had bypassed Jez. He was now an anachronism, a spirit out of time. He revelled in his exile from society and wore it as a badge of honour. He bore the burden of becoming a teacher and guide to Dog with great dignity.

"Dog." The second kick was harder than the first and more accurately aimed, striking Dog in the centre of his back.

"Whaaa, wha's goin' on?"

Jez pulled hard on his recently rolled ciggie. He could feel the smoke working its way through his lungs. He knew if he concentrated hard enough, he would feel the nicotine seep into his bloodstream. He had the ability to understand and even control some of those inner forces, but right now, he couldn't be arsed and just enjoyed the smoke.

Dog struggled to get up. "What's with the aggression?"

"Here." Jez handed him the rollup.

"Ah, sound."

"How much have we got?"

"How much what?" Dog asked straining to get the last out the ciggie.

"Money. We've got to pool our resources to get out of here."

"Oh, yeah." Dog searched through his pockets, which was as long and laborious a project as it was for Jez. The result was a little more promising as he pulled out coins to the value of 72 pence.

"Shit, I need some food and energy, man, and soon."

"Hold on," Dog said. He pulled off his boot and rummaged around. Jez struggled with the pungent smell that wafted his way. *Ammonia? Sweat?* No, it was the smell of decay and the rich, damp culture of advancing fungi.

"Shit, you could grow mushrooms in those socks."

"Nah, something more valuable here," Dog declared. "What do you think of that?" Dog held up a battered ten-pound note.

"I think you're well on the way to becoming a true Mudda," Jez said.

"What's a Moo-da?" Dog asked, scratching his chin.

"Someone like me, who represents the culmination of scientific thought in Marxism, fused with the spiritual understanding of Buddhism."

Dog didn't understand what Jez was on about. He would try to remember what seemed to be keywords to be dropped in at what seemed to be appropriate points, but somehow, he never got it right. He handed the tenner over. His trust in Jez was unwavering. It wasn't something he thought about. It was natural. Jez was his brother. Not a brother with the same mum, but better. Jez had never put his head down a toilet and pulled the chain, nor had he pulled his trousers down in front of girls. Jez wouldn't do that because he was a real brother.

"How did we get here?" Dog asked.

"It is enough to know that all roads lead to the present. Everything was predetermined to lead us here, and from here to wherever we are due next."

"Where's that?" Dog asked expectantly.

"Depends where we get a lift to." Jez crammed his old sleeping bag into a backpack. "Come on, let's get moving. See if we can find a way out of here."

They were at the entrance to a service station, and despite the temptation of Dog's ten pound seventy-two pence, Jez led the way through the car park, passing the restaurant on through the petrol station to the start of the slip road.

After half an hour of indifferent hitch-hiking, Dog was tiring. Jez sat on the ground, resting against his backpack.

"Is it my turn to sit down yet?" Dog asked.

"Yeah, no problem," Jez said while rolling his second

ciggie of the day. "But we agreed to do an hour each, and you have only done half of yours. Do another half hour, then we can swap."

"But we haven't got a watch."

"Don't you trust me?"

"Yeah, of course, I do." Dog declared.

"Then, don't panic. I'll let you know when the hour's up."

"Yeah, okay. Man, I hope someone stops soon. If I had a car, I'd stop and give people lifts. Why won't anyone give us a lift?"

"The thing is there's no respect for real travellers anymore: nomads, free spirits, people unchained and unfettered by the daily grind of capitalism..."

"Is that why no one is giving us a lift— 'cos they're capitalists?"

"It's because they are miserable bastards."

"Hey, look, a wagon." Dog pointed at a blue transit van that was pulling into the service station car park. "They must be travellers too. Let's go and check."

"Whoooaaa, hold on there. Look at them—they're not travellers. They're scallies. You have to be careful around people like that."

Dog wasn't put off. "Come on, they might give us a lift. Look, one of them has got a dog. They can't be that bad." He turned his good ear toward the van, "And they're playing Motorhead. Come on." Dog was on his way across the car park.

"Wait, hold on. You don't know anything about them. It

could be a trap."

The comment made Dog stop. "Who'd want to trap us?"

"New laws, the establishment, and the Masons…all those people—they're all threatened by tribes."

Dog didn't have a clue what Jez was on about, but it felt serious.

"Better let me lead this one." Jez strode forward, Dog following a few paces behind. They dodged the cars leaving the petrol station, trying to keep out of view.

"Did you see how many there were?"

"I saw three or four and the dog."

"And they all went into the cafe?" Jez asked.

"Yeah."

"Okay," said Jez. "Here's what we're going to do. You go toward the van acting naturally, don't draw attention to yourself, then try the van door to see if it's open. I'll be watching out for you from over here."

"I'm not sure," Dog said. "Can't we just ask them for a lift?"

"What's wrong with you? I've just explained why we can't do that."

Dog shrugged. "Yeah, okay."

"Go on, then, move! I'll wait here for you."

Dog walked between the parked cars, his heavy boots crunching on the gravel. *Act naturally*, he thought, so he swung his arms in pretence of normality, his legs lifting high, body responding to the rhythmic beat in his head. *Yeah, cool, no problem.*

Jez winced as he watched Dog bouncing like a puppet,

arms and legs controlled by invisible strings, orange head bobbing up and down. Dog turned back to Jez and gave him a thumbs up.

Dog was concentrating on 'acting naturally' and giving the thumbs up to Jez when a Ford Sierra came skidding to a stop. The driver was astonished to see this orange-haired zombie step out in front of him.

Through his open window, the driver shouted, "Fucking idiot."

His wife tried to calm him down. "Gary, keep quiet. He might be on drugs."

"On drugs? He's lucky he's not on the fucking bonnet." He threw a final "wanker" at Dog before restarting his engine.

Jez held his head in his hands. He would have to lose this guy and soon. This was embarrassing. When he looked up again, Dog was holding open the van door and waving wildly at him. He looked around to see if anyone else was watching Dog. There were a few people around, but nobody seemed to be taking any notice. Jez straightened up and walked quickly toward Dog and the van, his head looking from side to side, ready to break into a run should he need to escape.

"Okay, go on, get in," Jez ordered as he rushed round to the driver's side.

"Are we robbing it?" Dog asked as he climbed into the passenger seat.

"No, just sort of...liberating it." Jez had his head under the dashboard and was pulling away at the steering column. There was a sharp crack as the plastic cover of the steering column broke, revealing a mass of twisted multicoloured cables. Jez expertly isolated and stripped two cables. He touched them together, and the starter motor churned away for ten seconds before spluttering to a halt. "Come on, you bastard." Jez touched the wires for a second time producing a more robust but no more effective noise.

"Shit."

"Maybe it doesn't want to be liberated?"

The searing look from Jez was enough to silence Dog.

"This time. Come. On."

The starter motor turned, once, twice, and then with his foot down on the accelerator, Jez felt the engine engage with a roar. After he threw it into first gear, the van kangaroo-ed forward. Jez and Dog cheered its jerky movement.

"We're away. Turn the music on.," Jez shouted in celebration.

Dog fumbled with the radio switch until a suitable assault could be found for the eardrums. Once found, the electric cords accompanied their escape from the car park. Jez took the turning for the service station exit and was soon out into the flow of the traffic.

***

Kevin allowed Susan to run on. Sandy did his best to run but trailed behind on his lead. "Come on, Sandy…" Sandy had given up running a long time ago and wasn't about to start again now. Susan let the lead drop. "Kev, can you grab the dog?"

"Here, come on, boy." Kevin did his best to cajole Sandy. Unimpressed, Sandy sat down.

Susan burst into the restaurant and ran to where Renie and Vinny were sat.

"Nan, you'd better come outside."

"Why, what's going on?"

"Just come out, will you." Susan reached down and began pulling at her coat.

"Give over, child."

Kevin had appeared at the door and held it open.

Susan's voice was getting more desperate. "Come on, then."

Renie sensed the urgency, "Is it that, Kevin? If he's done anything to you, I'll cut his balls off."

Kevin leant down and whispered to Sandy. "Chance would be a fine thing."

"No, Nan, it's the van," Susan explained.

"What about the van?" Vinny started getting up.

"It's gone," Susan announced. "Someone's robbed it."

Kevin was motioning at the door for Vinny to join him.

There was a screech from Renie somewhere between a cry of pain and a moan of exasperation, and then, in calmer but more horrified tones, she asked, "What about Jack?"

"Wait here." Vinny slid out from behind the table. "I'm going to call the police."

Susan took his place next to Renie and put a comforting hand on her arm. "Don't worry. I'm sure they'll find him."

Kevin went inside with the dog.

"What's going on?" John had made his way over, followed by Liam.

"Here, I'll take Sandy." Liam reached out to take the

lead from Kevin. "Thanks for looking after him, son."

"No problem," Kevin replied.

"Is someone gonna tell me what's going or what?" John raised his voice to make himself heard.

"Someone's robbed the van," Susan repeated.

"Oh, shit."

"Yeah," Kevin said, "and I think the dog just has."

Vinny came back in. "I've been on the police. They should be here in a couple of minutes."

"Did you lock it?" John asked Vinny.

"How could I?" Vinny replied. "You lot were still in the back."

"For fuck's sake," John said.

"Don't you blame him." Renie spoke up for Vinny. "If you weren't drinking all night, you wouldn't have been asleep in the back."

"Ooow! Dad, Sandy's dropped one," Ian complained.

Customers on the surrounding tables had begun to notice a smell that they suspected had nothing to do with their hamburgers. Noses were wrinkled and were eyebrows raised as Sandy sat down to begin his midday ablutions.

"Dad, look, he's licking his balls now. Why is he doing that?"

"Ian, will you shut up a minute," Renie snapped.

"Because he can," Kevin quipped in answer to Ian.

"What did the police say?" asked John.

"They've got a car in the area. They should be here in a minute."

"Did you tell them about Jack?" asked Renie.

"No. How do you explain you've lost a dead body?" Vinny held his hands up in exasperation.

"Who the hell is desperate enough to steal a van with a body in it?" asked John.

Ian hadn't seen this much excitement since the fight at his cousin's wedding. "Could 've been the bodysnatchers."

"Excuse me, sir."

The assistant manager had made his way back over and interrupted John's train of thought. "What do you want?" John snapped.

"It's the dog, sir. The rules."

"What? What the fuck are you on about?" It was clear John was beginning to fray at the edges.

"There's no need for that kind of language," Renie scolded.

"I'm sorry, but I'm going to have to get the Manager." The assistant hastily retreated.

Everyone was crowded around a single table. No one knew what to do. Things had quietened down, and the shock of the theft sank in. After a few minutes, Kevin got up and wandered outside, closely followed by Susan.

From a door to the left of the food counter, the assistant manager emerged, followed by the manager, who distinguished by his lack of red and white uniform, his sign of office being its absence. His walk from his office to the site of the problem was confident and purposeful. He was on familiar ground here. John had started pacing up and down, and it was while pacing that he saw Susan and Kevin kissing just outside the main door. "Hey," he shouted, "Don't you think we've got enough going on? Get back in here."

"Sorry, dad." Susan apologised as she pulled herself away from Kevin.

"What the hell's going on?" John said to himself. He could feel his world slipping out of kilter.

It was just at that moment the manager arrived. He pulled the assistant manager back and stepped forward, placing himself directly in front of John. If he had any fear, he hid it well, which was more than could be said for his assistant, who cowered behind him. The manager was a tall man in his early thirties. He had years of amateur rugby behind him. His stature and confidence were usually enough to bring second thoughts to any mischievous minds, a useful attribute given his location between Liverpool and North Wales. "Is there a problem here?" he asked.

"And who the hell are you?"

"I'm the manager, and I'm asking you to take the animal, and please, leave the restaurant."

John stood his ground and stared at the manager.

It was an unsettling experience for the manager. It wasn't the face, itself enough to shake the confidence of most, nor the eyes that were fixed, immovable—it was the knowledge that the man in front of him would stop at nothing. His sense was that this man was able to cross the line between the rational and the insane with impunity.

"I'm the manager, and I'm asking you to take the animal, and please leave the restaurant," he repeated.

John knew the voice lacked the authority of the frame.

Liam spoke up, "It's okay. The dog's mine. I'll take it

out."

"No, you won't, Liam. You stay where you are."

"Take the dog out." Renie broke the stalemate. She knew what John was like when something got him started. Liam led Sandy toward the main door.

"Thank you," the manager said, trying to hide his relief.

"Is that how you get your kicks? Ordering old men around?"

"John, leave it be," Renie snapped.

"Is there a problem here?" a voice called from the front door. It was the second time John had heard the phrase in a couple of minutes.

"Yeah, we seem to have a fucking parrot in the room." John turned to face two policemen who had just entered the restaurant.

"Is everything okay here?" Charlie, the taller of the two officers, addressed the question to the manager, whose shirt and tie clearly marked him out as the ally of law and order.

"Yes, officer, everything is fine now."

"We have had a report of a stolen vehicle?" the second shorter officer added.

"That was from me." Vinny stood up.

The shorter officer, Terry, encouraged the group of curious customers that were gathering to disperse.

"It's a blue Ford transit. It was parked right outside."

"Registration?" asked Charlie.

"Yeah, here it is," Vinny said as he was checking his documents, "X456 SMJ."

"Right, I'll radio that in," Charlie said in his thick Welsh accent. "If we're lucky, someone will pick them up pretty soon. They won't have gotten far. Probably on their way to Liverpool."

"That's right," the manager said, "most crime round here is committed by Scousers."

Charlie nodded. "Well known fact, it is," he added.

"Should just put a border crossing down the road, save a lot of trouble that would," Terry said. "I'll be radioing it in, now." He shook his radio as proof. Then, he pressed the button, and a loud crackle broke through the air. He winked at Vinny and pressed again. "Delta, Hotel One, DH 1…" The radio crackled, and another voice could be heard. Terry moved away from the group. "Eleven twenty-five, repeat 11-25…"

Vinny couldn't quite hear the voice coming back through, but there was a lot of roger this and roger that.

"Tell him about Jack," Renie interrupted. "Make sure you tell him."

"Who's Jack?" Charlie, the taller policeman, asked.

Terry, the smaller officer, had returned. "Does someone mind explaining to me what's going on?"

"He was in the van," Vinny said.

"Jack was in the van when it was robbed," Ian added.

Terry's eyes widened, and his eyebrows rose. "In the van he was? When it was stolen, was it?"

"Yeah…but you don't understand," said Vinny.

Terry didn't look pleased. "All done, mate. Reported it in I 'ave."

"You keep an eye on these by 'ere, Terry. It's not an 11-24 mate. What we've got here is an 11-8." Charlie, realising the seriousness of the situation and not wanting to be outdone by his colleague, got on his radio.

Terry was upset that it would look like he had radioed in the wrong information. "11-8. That'a wounded animal. We haven't got that?" He looked at John. "Did they hurt the dog when they took the van?"

John shook his head, confused. "No, what…"

"Not a kick or anything?" he asked.

Renie spoke up. "We told your mate here that there is someone in the van."

"Yeah," It suddenly clicked for Terry. "11-8's an abduction. We don't get many of them round by 'ere."

Exasperated, John appealled to Vinny. "Jesus, can you explain to dumb and dumber here what happened."

"Look, can you get your mate off the radio for a minute?" Vinny asked.

Terry resisted. "We got to report it in, mate, first thing we have to do. How old was the person in the van?"

"I don't know, 60's…late 60's, but you don't understand."

"He's dead," Ian cut in.

Terry's jaw dropped. He lifted his cap and wiped his brow. "Oh, my goodness, now, dead, you say?" His eyes widened as he asked.

"Charlie. Charlie, mate." He waved to get his colleague's attention. Charlie broke his radio contact and snapped at Terry. "We gotta get this in, mate. They'll have regional crime squad on this they will."

"Fuck regional crime squad. This Jack they are on

about...is dead."

"Oh, shit," Charlie exclaimed. "How do you know?"

"He was dead before the van was stolen," Vinny explained.

***

Liam stepped out into the daylight and walked with Sandy to a small patch of grass that lined the car park. Sandy lay on the cool ground, and Liam bent down slowly to give him a pat. Sandy's tail gave a tired wag. It was hard for Liam to sit down on the grass. His old bones were not as agile as they used to be. He stroked Sandy.

"Jack would've loved all this, you know. He was a rum bugger. He's probably up there now having a good laugh at this mess."

Sandy flicked his head. Liam closed his eyes and relaxed in the cool air.

The business of the service station continued uninterrupted. Cars containing families, lovers, and even enemies came and went—journeys interrupted, delayed, and resumed.

Liam opened his eyes to green and brown shapes swimming in front of him, sending his head spinning as a military vehicle drew up.

Where the hell am I? He reached out and felt Sandy next to him. Swinging his head from side to side, he realised he was still in the car park. *Christ, that gave me a fright.* Sandy snuggled closer.

A troop carrier parked right in front of Liam and began

to dispatch its load. The soldier who climbed out first looked fit and healthy, his closely cropped hair covered by a black beret pulled down on one side, fatigues matching the vehicle. The soldier shone with life. His eyes were bright and clear, white teeth and unblemished skin. Others evacuated the carrier, and a small group laughed and joked. These youth trained to kill others were comfortable in themselves and life. Liam looked beyond the uniforms to the innocence and individuality of a deadly force—a unit that was innocent until it was used.

***

"We did it, man. We did it!"

With music blaring and the afternoon sun shining, they were really on their way. This was more like it. Sod all that waiting about. Why hitch when the world is overpopulated with cars? It would teach them a lesson anyway—they shouldn't have left it unlocked.

Dog was happy because Jez seemed happy.

"I helped, didn't I, Jez?"

"Dog...you were wicked."

Dog beamed with pride. His world was never better than at this moment, except maybe that one time at school when the teacher hung one of his paintings on the wall. Even then, some of the kids had called him a creep, so this was definitely better.

Jez was thinking ahead. "We should get off this main road. The filth will be looking for us."

"Jez...you'd better have a look at this."

"Look at what? I'm driving."

"Jez…there's a coffin in the back."

Jez manoeuvred the rear-view mirror to look into the back of the van. He could see a patch of wood but couldn't make out the shape. "It's probably just an orange box or something."

"It's not for carrying oranges, Jez. I think we should stop."

"Fuck. I can't stop here."

Since seeing the coffin, Dog kept his eyes firmly on the road ahead. "Turn off the road. We need to stop."

"Hey, since when do you decide what we do?"

"I don't like it. It makes me feel funny. I mean…what if it's got a body in it?"

"You're only worried because you've never been near another body, alive or dead, especially the female ones. Hey, maybe it's your lucky day, and there's a female stiff in there. A female stiff for your stiffy…hey, get it?"

"That's not funny."

"There's no body in there. It's just a wooden box. Chill out."

"Here, there's a turning. Please, Jez."

"Alright...Alright." Jez pulled the van into the nearside lane. "You know bodies aren't important anyway. What's important is the spirit, the essence. This exists above and beyond the flesh."

"You mean like ghosts?" Dog started biting his nails.

"No…ghosts are bullshit. The elites can't control the

spirits, the essence of things, so they make it like a Disneyland. The haunted house, ghost train, and all that crap. They turn everything into commodities. They prostitute and monetise it. Real spirituality comes from within and then exudes without. I would call it Karma, but fucking hippies have ruined that word. Anyway, the point is you don't have to worry about the body."

Jez slowed down the van as they came to a slip road. Dog tried to ignore the scraping noise of the coffin as the road took a sharp curve to the left. The road straightened out onto a roundabout.

"We'll take the small road," said Jez. "Less chance of being spotted."

"Yeah, good. Are we going to ditch the van?"

"Nah…but, we will pull over and just make sure there's nothing in the box, just to calm you down."

"No, no…we can't do that, Jez. We might disturb the spirits."

Jez pulled the van over onto a grass verge. They were hidden from the main road by a hedge, so the place was secure.

"By the look of the scallies that got out of this van, there's no worries on that score. To have a spirit, you have got to have done something in life. If there is anyone in there…" He threw his head backwards toward the coffin. "…all they will have done is dragged their sad arses to work every day. Just one more member of the zombie nation. Right, this should do." He turned the engine off and opened the door. "Come on, let's get this thing open."

Dog sat rigid. Jez pulled the handbrake on, unbuckled his seatbelt, and jumped out of the open door. He was round at the back of the van before Dog started to move. When he did move, Dog took a position about five feet behind Jez, well away from the van. Jez pulled the handle down and yanked the door open. Dog felt the metal screech as vibrations passed through his bones.

"Shit, it's Aladdin's cave in here. Look at this booze." Jez threw a can to Dog. "Get your laughing gear round that." Jez climbed in the van, unscrewed the top off a bottle of lemonade, and wafted it under his nose. He raised it to his mouth and took a big gulp. "Man, that's good stuff."

"What is it?" Dog had opened the lager, and his resistance to entering the van again was weakening. "What is it?" he repeated.

"Here, come and get it."

Dog stepped forward.

"Finest produce of the proletarian state. Vodka, or should I say *Wodka,* komrade!"

"Yeah, that's good." Dog wiped his mouth. He moved closer and began filling his pockets with cans of beer.

"Old Joe Stalin had the right idea. Give the masses enough cheap vodka, and you can get away with murder." Jez opened a can of lager, and the head foamed out of the can and dripped down to form a small pool on the coffin surface. "Do you think he drinks Carling Black Label?" Dog was into his second drink of vodka when Jez reached out and grabbed the bottle off him. "Thanks for saving me some, you greedy bastard."

"I would've given it back," Dog protested, then returned in disappointment to his lager.

"How brave are you feeling then?" asked Jez.

"What for?"

Jez sat astride the coffin placing his can on the floor beside him. "Just to show you, there's nothing in here." He started working one of the screws with the ring pull from his can.

"No, Jez, this isn't funny."

"I'm just gonna have a look."

Dog stepped back away from the van. "Leave it, eh." His head hung low, and his fingers furiously twirled loose threads from his jacket.

"We'll just have a look." Jez threw a screw from the coffin toward Dog, who caught it instinctively before realising what it was and letting it fall to the ground.

He'd had enough now. Still carrying his can, Dog turned and walked off up the road. *I don't need this; it's not right. Why should he tell me what to do all the time? I looked after myself before he came along. I can do it again.* His resolution made, he marched on, turning his head every thirty seconds to see if Jez was following him. He wasn't. *Fuck him and all his shit.*

Walking toward the roundabout, Dog was determined to start hitchhiking when he saw the police. The patrol car came down the same slip road Jez and Dog had come off twenty minutes earlier. It turned onto the roundabout. Dog crouched down. The police car didn't turn off but began coming round again.

"Shit." Dog dived into a ditch beside the road. His can of lager went flying, and he ended up lying face down in a puddle of muddy water. As the cold, dirty water soaked through his clothes, he felt like a cold, greasy hand was giving him a rub down.

"Shit."

After what seemed like ages, Dog raised his head to road level; they'd gone. He climbed out onto the road and started running back to the van. His wet clothes were slapping against his body. The cans of lager were bumping and bouncing at every step. He started unloading the cans, and they flew off him in all directions as he ran.

Arriving back at the van, his face streaked with mud and breathless, he managed to speak.

"Jez, it's the police."

Still working away at the screws, Jez looked up. "What the fuck happened to you?"

"It's the police. They were up at the roundabout."

Jez threw the ring pull away. A look of fear flashed over this face. "Did they see you?"

"No, I don't think so, but we'd better get out of here. They must be looking for the van."

Jez regained his composure. "Yeah, I suppose you're right." He tossed his can over his shoulder toward the front seat. "What shall we take: the money or the box? Deal or no deal?"

"What?" Dog started moving.

"Never mind. You just don't understand, do you? Come on. We'll go across the fields 'till we get a few miles away."

***

The scene was one of relief all around, as the van, complete with coffin and passengers, pulled out of the restaurant car park, escorted by a police car, and waved off by the restaurant manager.

"Did they get the bastards?" asked John.

"No, but they got their descriptions," Vinny shouted.

"The bastards got my vodka as well."

Renie snapped at John. "Do you mind cutting out the language? Getting your vodka was probably the only good thing to happen."

"Two punks according to the police," continued Vinny.

"That makes sense: no taste, no style, who else would rob a van with a coffin in it?"

Susan gave Kevin's hand a squeeze before joining the discussion herself. "Yeah, they must be sick."

"They will be now if they drank my vodka. 90 percent proof it was. Real communist rotgut. That stuff could've brought the Berlin wall down on its own," John quipped.

"Hey, look," Ian shouted while standing and pointing out the front. "We've got a police escort."

John reached out, and while pulling Ian back down, asked, "So what did they look like, these punk rockers?"

"The only thing they told me was that one of them had orange hair," answered Vinny.

"Renie, how did you get on with the phone call?"

"Oh, yeah, sorry. I meant to tell you. They've spoken to the priest, and they will go ahead with the service today, and they will rearrange the internment for tomorrow morning."

"Well, they can't do the burial without the body, so they'll have to wait."

"If you have to be so ignorant," Renie continued to John, "Do you have to do it in front of the children?"

John responded to the rebuke by opening his only remaining can of beer and staring pointedly out of the rear window.

"I've arranged for somewhere to stay for us all. It will only be sofas and the floor, but we'll manage."

Susan and Kevin sought out each other's eyes at the mention of the overnight stay. The warmth that passed between them was so strong it was physical for Kevin. Susan's face flushed as she anticipated the night ahead. She looked as pretty as anyone Kevin had ever seen.

"Are they going all the way with us?" Ian asked. "I bet you usually have them behind you chasing, not in front." Tickled by his joke, Ian broke into a fit of giggles.

"He's a rum bugger," Liam chuckled.

"He is that." John smiled.

"Little bugger," Renie added, her face broadening into a smile of pride.

Susan gave Kevin's hand a squeeze. Vinny couldn't help smiling to himself. He was beginning to identify with these people. *Yeah, Kev might be right that they are all mad, but who the fuck could blame them?*

Vinny knew he had a way out. This trip was part of it. Doing this would keep him in his lecturer's good books. He would scrape through with a degree in History and Social Studies. It wasn't that he wanted a degree. University had just become a way to get off the estate. He wasn't sure what he would do, but he knew he wouldn't end up dead in the back of a van being driven across the country. He struggled with University but not because of the work—he could handle that. He was surrounded by the sons and daughters of accountants and lawyers. He felt out of place. He went back to Speke as little as possible. It was empty for him, like the father he never knew, an ex who wanted nothing to do with him, a son he would probably never know. His life wasn't tidy. Christ, they didn't know the half of things. It wasn't that he didn't like his lecturers and the other students, but they didn't know what real life was. But then again, neither do I, he thought. I left. Back for one day in a van, and all of a sudden, I'm an expert.

***

"Back to square-fucking-one. No man, it's even worse than that. Back to the square fucking root of one." Jez threw the last of his lager cans into the air. He watched it swirling through the air droplets, spinning off against the blue of the afternoon sky. "Half an hour ago, we had a van, music, and booze, and we were putting the miles behind us. Now we are stuck in the middle of sheep shagging land, walking. Here we are in the twenty-first century, and we are using the oldest form of transport known to man."

"Yea, well, at least we don't have a dead body with us, and we're not being chased by the police." Dog was stepping out into the grass, enjoying the warm air and the absence of both van and coffin. "Hey, look, this ain't so bad." Dog pointed out into the countryside. "We've even got wildlife."

"Dog…they're sheep. Sheep aren't wildlife. They're walking cardigans and Sunday dinners. Can't you see the mint sauce coming out of its arse?"

Dog didn't talk for a while after this. Jez did. In fact, Dog thought Jez would never shut up. He went on and on. Dog had stopped listening a while ago, and instead, concentrated on each step he took. He was trying to avoid the muddy bits as they crossed another field, aiming for the tufts of grass in between the muddy ground. It wasn't too bad like this as long as he stared at his feet and didn't think about how far he was going. In fact, it was soothing watching one muddy boot after the other. Dog could even imagine that they weren't his boots. They could belong to a soldier in Afghanistan, fighting the "Tally bans" in a war he didn't really know what it was all about. But he knew they were fighting. No one had ever fought for them when his mother had no money for food or for school uniforms. Why did people have to go all over the world to fight when they could fight for things here?

He knew Jez was still talking, and every now and again, he said, "Yeah." He didn't know what he was saying "yeah" to, but it seemed to keep Jez happy.

The next road they came to didn't offer much hope of a lift, but it was the only hope they had. "Walk or hitch?" asked Dog.

"Doesn't look like we've got much choice, does it?" Jez was pointing away down the deserted road. They walked in single file along the tarmac. There wasn't much to look at or hitch a lift from. Cars were coming through at the rate of one every five minutes. None stopped. After a period of extended silence, Dog asked, "Jez, does it bother you?"

"You bother me with your constant whining."

"No, I mean like death. Like that body in the coffin. Does it scare you?"

"No, it doesn't scare me. Do you know why?" He stopped walking and turned to face Dog. "Because I won't know about it. I'll be dead. Won't I, dickhead?" He turned and started walking again.

This time there was a five-minute gap before Dog spoke again. "That's what scares me." Jez didn't answer and continued walking.

"Not knowing anything, not feeling, not being able to think."

Jez stopped again. "Then it will make no fucking difference to you then, will it? Now shut the fuck up, and let's concentrate on getting out of here."

"If I could be a hero, though, or do some really brilliant invention, then it wouldn't be like I was dead because people would still talk about me like I was alive. They would say, 'Oh that Dog was a brave bastard, did you hear what he did when…'"

Jez interrupted. "Go on then, when he did...what?"

"Well, when I did whatever it was that made me a hero…or an inventor…or…is love like that? Do you think that is what they mean?"

Jez couldn't believe his luck when he saw a car approaching. "Get your thumb out, come on."

The mini indicated and pulled over. They both ran to catch it. Dog was first to the door and opened it, only to be pulled back by Jez. The driver leaned over the passenger seat. "Where are you boys going?"

"Erhh...where are you going?" Jez asked.

"Anglesey," he answered.

"That's great," said Jez. "Never been there."

***

They had found Amlwch by driving round Anglesey for an hour. The island was a web of small roads between tiny hamlets and towns. White painted houses offset the local grey stone and the dark greens and browns of the local vegetation. The main problem wasn't geography but understanding the accents of the locals when they stopped for directions. The island itself is the heartland of the Welsh language, and the place names were unpronounceable for a group of weary travellers from Liverpool.

The van spluttered and coughed its way into the small town on the Irish Sea coast of Anglesey.

"Bull Bay Road," Renie announced.

"Woah, look at that." Vinny pulled the van over the side of the road.

The van had stopped next to a strange building that announced itself as Our Lady of The Sea and St Winifred.

"Why are we stopping?" Kevin asked.

"We're here. Well, it's got to be close. This place is tiny. And look at that." Vinny was pointing through the windscreen.

"We are here!" Renie said, "You're right. This is the church."

"Okay, come on, everyone out."

The van emptied in seconds. Everyone was glad at the chance to stretch their legs.

"This is the road," Renie announced.

"Why don't you go on ahead, give them some warning, then come back and get us," suggested Vinny.

"Will do," said Renie. "John, you're with me. Susan, keep Ian out of trouble 'till we get back, will you."

"Yeah, Nan."

Liam took the chance to walk Sandy into the churchyard.

Vinny's eyes followed the shape of the church. The church was concrete rather than stone, but it was its unusual shape that drew Vinny's attention. The roof was arched, with ribs set along its length. Under each rib were round windows, and the entrance door was set high, reached by a staircase from both sides. The window above the main entrance was in the shape of a star.

"I've got it."

"Got what?" Kevin asked.

"The church, can you see what it is?"

"Yeah, a church. The church is a church; what a shock." Kevin shrugged his shoulders at Susan. "Come on, shall we go and have a look?"

"No," Vinny called after them. "It's a ship."

"Look, Ian, can you see how if you turned the church upside down, it would be a ship?"

Ian looked a little confused but nonetheless agreed. Then he had his own moment of revelation. "Yeah, I get it. The windows are round."

"Portholes," said Vinny.

"That's cool."

"Yeah, you know what…it is."

The Connolly's house, home to the deceased, was a small brick terrace. A two-up, two-down of the type destroyed by most urban councils in the slum clearances of the 60s. Amlwch had never been fortunate enough to suffer a slum clearance of this type. The home of the Connolly's was built by the owners of the copper mine that became the economic foundation of the town.

It wasn't until Vinny entered the house that the real nature of their journey struck him. In the dimly lit room with closed curtains, there were two candlesticks on the mantelpiece with candles burned halfway down. The muffled sobs of the old people sat around the walls of the room in straight back chairs, provided a constant hum. The semi-darkness and the smell of the candles indicated the unmistakable presence of death. The centre of the room was empty except for two trestles placed approximately four feet apart.

Mrs Connolly, the widow of the deceased, embraced Renie. The rest of the passengers shifted nervously behind Vinny. The two women embraced, a wife and a sister connected through one man. The embrace was acknowledgement of the other's right to grieve. When the women parted, Jack's widow took her place in a seat against the wall, and Renie left the room to supervise the introduction of the coffin.

Vinny and Kevin helped to carry the coffin in. The

weight of the coffin and the physicality of it caused it to scrape over trestles as the two men maneuvered it into place. It stood in contrast to the religious aura of burning candles, darkness, and muttered prayers.

"Thank God, a bit of fresh air."

"I know what you mean," Susan smiled at Kevin.

Sandy must have recognised the warmth in Kevin's voice because the dog snuggled his head against Kevin's leg. "That mutt is turning out to be a blessing in disguise.

Come on, then, let's give this guy his walk."

"Which way?" asked Susan.

"Down," Kevin answered, pointing. "We came in that way, so we know there's jack squat up there."

They followed the slight incline down the terraced street. Susan led the dog, and Kevin was at her side.

The only conversation between them was to decide on turnings as they approached the end of the narrow streets. Before long, they found themselves at the side of the harbour and docks. For a small town, the dockside was impressive, stretching out along the harbour with at least three stone or concrete jetties pushing out into the sea.

"I could never live here. This place is so depressing."

"Depends what you are used to." Susan lifted her head, facing into the cold wind that was blowing in off the sea. "This is nice."

"This is fucking freezing."

"Yeah, I know," Susan said, "but listen."

Kevin made a show of listening, lifting his hand to his ear. "What for?"

"The sea. Can't you hear it?"

"Yeah...but it's fucking freezing. Can't we go back?"

"Okay, but it's just so different, look...just look out there, miles and miles of water, so much space. Kev, where are your family from?"

"Toxteth."

"No, I mean, at some point, they must've come from somewhere else."

"Yeah, Barbados. My grandad was on the boats, got to Liverpool in...the twenties, I think."

"Same as mine then."

"What...from Barbados?" Kevin was smiling.

"No, stupid, the sea. Except he was Irish."

"Sue, I'm not being funny. This is a very interesting conversation and all that, but I think my dick has just snapped off; it's so fucking cold."

"Well, I hope not." This time Susan was smiling. "You wouldn't be much good to me without it."

They started walking back to the house. A lingering kiss beside the harbour had finally confirmed what each had been hoping.

"Hey, you!"

They were just about to turn into the street where Mrs Connolly lived.

"You, nigger."

Susan grabbed Kevin's arm. "Don't turn around. Come on, we're nearly there."

Kevin kept walking but turned to see three guys on the other side of the street. They were in their twenties, wearing the uniform of scallies, trackies, and trainers. They were fairly well built. He'd noticed them as he walked up the street with Susan. It was natural for him to weigh people up, especially in white areas. Most of the time, it was unconscious, but he was well outside his normal territory, so had been on guard since they had arrived.

"Fuck you." He threw back at them.

Susan was pulling him up the street. "Don't let them bother you."

"Stop pulling me, ok? And yeah, I will let it bother me. You want me to ignore them? Let the bastards get away with it?"

Susan dropped his arm. "I didn't mean it like that," she protested.

Kevin carried on walking. "Well, don't worry. What can I do with three of the bastards?"

They continued up the street to the house. The anger in each, though aimed at the racists, deflected a little at the other in frustration at not being able to do anything about it.

***

"What do you reckon then?" Kevin asked as they walked into the pub.

"There's not a lot we can do. We're here now." Vinny shrugged in resignation.

Set back off the road, a once-proud hotel, The Liverpool Arms, shouted its attractions in fluorescent pink and green. Cottage pies and happy hour were the current attractions.

At seven o'clock, the bar was empty. The absence of

music, bar staff, or customers only added to the sense of the unreal that had followed Vinny all day. The polished tables, perfectly spaced beer mats, and fresh, clean light that poured in the bay windows behind him prepared his mind for the bizarre.

"Beetlejuice."

"No, beer lager, bitter mild, even a short, but I'm pretty sure they won't serve…"

Kevin didn't get a chance to finish.

"No, *Beetlejuice*, the film. You know where everything seems out of place, or anything can happen, like a giant snake sliding up to serve us, or when I blink, I'll be in the deep end of a swimming pool. Don't you ever get that feeling?"

"Yeah, definitely a short." Kevin walked to the end of the bar looking around for bar staff. "I think this trip is getting to you."

"You might be right." Rummaging in his pockets for change, Vinny walked over to the jukebox. His pound coin slid into the opening, making a series of metallic clicks.

Kevin joined him. "What do you reckon to Suzie then?"

"Oh, gimme a break, Kev. It's not truly, madly, deeply already, is it?"

Kevin looked around, despite knowing the room was empty. "No, but she's okay."

The jukebox kicked in, and the opening notes of 'Brown Eyed Girl' began filling the room, seeping into the void of atmosphere.

"Evening." Attracted by the sound of music, a barmaid appeared. "Sorry, I was in the back."

Vinny approached the bar. "No problem."

Slowly the pub began to fill, a customer here, a couple there. People drifted through the frosted glass door. Each new person took out a section of emptiness, tables sprouted lives, and drinks disappeared down thirsty gullets. The music now mingled with the rising tide of voices, in whispers, confidently and confidentially, in earnest and laughter. They merged to form a part of the unmistakable atmosphere of a Saturday night.

Kevin and Vinny sat at a table while the rest of the male contingent that had left Liverpool that morning were stood at the bar.

"Is there a problem?" Vinny asked Kevin.

Kevin nodded toward a table, the other side of the room. A man in his late twenties or early thirties sat alone.

"He looks out of place," said Kevin.

Taking a second look, Vinny could see what Kevin meant. There was nothing in his dress that marked him out. He was well built and moderately good-looking, but he had a face that tells you to keep a distance, intelligent but hard. The man stood and walked to the bar. Kevin and Vinny watched as he ordered a pint and returned to his seat.

"Not our business." Vinny raised his pint and took a drink. "The world and all its problems end here for me." He drained his glass. "God, that was good."

Kevin took his and Vinny's glass and made his way to the bar. John was being served when Kevin joined him. John insisted on buying the round.

"Where are the women?"

"Where's Susan, you mean?" John gave him a dirty look.

Kevin responded defensively. "No, honest, I meant all them."

Liam slapped him on the back, "Don't worry, lad. He's taking the piss."

The object of Vinny and Kevin's curiosity had joined them at the bar. Closer up, Kevin couldn't discern any reason for his unease, but he still felt it. When the guy spoke, his voice was harsh. "Excuse me, Love, do you have a room for the night?" Kevin recognized the Northern Irish accent. It had the hard edge missing in the southern equivalent.

The barmaid was taken aback. "We do, but we only usually rent them out in the summer for walkers."

"Could you make one up for me?" the stranger asked.

"Of course. Give me a few minutes, and I'll sort it out for you."

"Thanks a lot," he said and returned to his table.

Kevin returned to Vinny, this time joined by John and Liam. The four men sat contemplating their beers.

"You're not local, are you?"

The question came from one of four young men on the next table.

"No," answered Vinny, "Liverpool."

"What are you here for?" The question seemed innocent enough to the four men.

"For a funeral." Vinny thought this information would at least announce their non-threatening presence in the pub. The youth, who asked, turned back to his friends and huddled over the table in conversation.

"Nosey bastard," said Kevin.

John leaned forward. "Yeah, well, in a place this small, everyone knows the smell of each other's farts."

"Same in Ireland," said Liam. "Jesus, you couldn't move in Wicklow without bumping into your mother's second cousin or your dad's auntie this or that. That was one of the things that made me move. The sense of freedom. Soon regretted it, though."

"Why?" asked Kevin.

"Well, it might seem like a pain at the time, but move away." He sighed before continuing. "You soon realize that there is no one to give a shit."

"Same as anywhere these days," said John. "Christ, some people are so desperate they would kick your teeth in for the change in your pocket."

The pub was as full as it would get on a Saturday night. Most of the tables were occupied, and there were half a dozen older men standing around the bar. The stranger who asked for the room had gone, although Vinny didn't notice him leave. His table was now taken by a middle-aged couple.

Liam insisted on buying drinks, so it was turning into a cheap night. Vinny was enjoying the chance to relax after the long drive.

"That must be Old Jack the Paddy?"

Vinny turned; the greasy-haired guy from the next table had asked the question. "Yeah, I guess so," he answered, "but if you don't mind, I'm with members of his family. So if you could show a bit of respect and let us have a drink in peace, eh?"

"Well said, son." John leaned over and gave Vinny a slap on the back.

The guys on the next table broke into laughter.

John had been staring hard at them. At the sound of laughter, he stood and walked over to stand in front of the guy who asked the question. The laughter died down and was replaced by silence. The questioner and obvious leader of the group stood to face John. Standing, he was of a similar height and build to John, but over twenty years younger. Vinny stood as well.

"Sit down, lad," Liam urged.

"Now, would you like to tell me what you found so funny about us being here to bury Jack Doyle?" John's stare hadn't shifted from the guy. His voice was calm and clear, and he looked relaxed.

The guy looked back to his friends for support as he continued. "Well, it was just that Jack Connolly was a Paddy, and we were wondering how many black Paddies there are?"

He turned back to John as he finished. The smile was still on his lips as John's forehead crashed into his face. His legs gave way as a spray of blood gushed from his burst nose. He lay on the floor, his choked moans gurgling through the blood in his mouth. Everyone and everything in the bar fell silent except the jukebox, which appropriately played the chorus to 'Another One Bites the Dust.' Without speaking, John reached down and grabbed the guy's jacket by the neck. Customers in the bar moved aside as John dragged him, still moaning to the door. He opened the door, dragged the bleeding youngster outside, and then came back in. A murmur of shocked voices grew as John marched to the table.

"You out," John said, pointing to the rest of the group.

Within seconds the table had cleared, and John was sitting back down.

"Fuck me," said Kevin. "I've never seen anything like that."

"It was bad enough them calling Uncle Jack a Paddy. I'd have done it for that alone," said John. "But you helped carry the coffin today, and I don't give a shite what color you are; that makes you one of us." He winked at Kevin, "At least for now, eh?"

***

The next day, the hearse didn't just look out of place in the narrow street. It looked like something from the movies. It was longer than the front of the house. Vinny was appointed a pallbearer, given the honor of a family member to someone he never knew. They'd accepted him and Kevin in a way that surprised him. The fight in the pub the previous night, the whiskeys, and handshakes around the coffin in the morning. These were special things, easily given, but no less meant or appreciated because of that. To be a part of them, it was necessary to be with them. Not to be like them, to agree with them, or to be one of them, but to share something with them. The recognition, respect, and solidarity of humanity. *To be with them.* He also knew that after this weekend, he would probably never see them again, but that was his life. It wasn't that this acceptance was unreal—just that he knew he didn't deserve it. He wouldn't be as faithful as they now believed he could be.

He had to remind himself that this was real. This weekend had been a reality in a way he had never quite grasped before. Maybe it was traveling with a body in the back of the van, but that was no longer true. It wasn't a body. Now, it was Jack, a guy he'd never met but whose weight he had felt. A guy who was loved by his family and died of a debilitating disease because he worked in an engine room forty years ago. A quiet family guy from a black and white photo with a bull neck. A guy who brought his niece presents from the sea and was leaving his best mate behind. It was somehow more real than anything he'd ever been through, and here was the shiny black car to take him to his grave.

"You okay?" Vinny asked as Kevin stepped out of the house.

"Yeah, I think so...fucking hillbillies, eh?" said Kevin.

"You know we're carrying him?" Vinny asked.

Kevin shrugged. "Yeah."

"Are you okay with it?"

"We've got to do what we got to do," Kevin answered.

"For fuck's sake, we're carrying this guy for his family. Don't do it if you don't want to."

Kevin's response was sharp. "Fuck you. I know what I'm doing, and if I didn't want to, I wouldn't, okay? So, don't give me any of your lectures…I am doing it."

"Alright, alright," Vinny said calmly.

The front door of the house opened behind Kevin.

"Are you lads ready? It's time." Renie had taken over

the arrangements. Her love for her lost brother would now be measured in the efficiency of his internment. "They're waiting inside."

Before he turned to enter the house, Vinny saw an orange head that was bobbing away up the street. He couldn't help but notice it—the contrast between the bobbing movement of this orange flash and the way everything else seemed to be operating at half speed in shades of grey.

As they turned the corner, Jez was the first to realize something was going on and did his thinking aloud. "What are these people hanging around for?"

Dog was too tired to even notice. "Jez, why couldn't we stay in the house last night?" Ignoring the people on doorsteps, Dog carried on. "It was smart in there, warm, and the bed was comfortable. Why couldn't we stay?"

Jez stopped Dog by putting his arm across his chest. "He wasn't trying to interfere with you, was he?"

"Well, how do you know he wasn't just being friendly. I mean, he did give us a meal, offer us a bed for the night. Better than sleeping in the fields."

Jez was staring hard at Dog. "I think the first clue I got was when he came into the bedroom and put his hand under the blanket and grabbed hold of me."

"Where?" asked Dog.

"Just fuck off, will you...you know you're pissing me off."

Dog didn't answer but started walking off. After a few yards, he turned to face Jez. When he spoke, it was with quiet determination. "You know, Jez, I don't need you."

Jez rushed to catch him up. "Hang on, Dog...I didn't mean it...Dog, I was only messing.."

Kevin and Vinny were on opposite sides of the coffin. John and Liam were at the back. It was strange, but even in the short distance from the room to the hearse, they fell into a marching step.

As they left the house, Vinny could see neighbors appearing from behind closed doors. It was as if a signal had been sent. The street was full of waiting people, watching as the coffin came out. Vinny aimed for the back of the hearse. They straightened up the coffin, ready to slide it into the hearse when it happened.

A man dressed in black stepped forward right in front of Vinny.

"Would you hold it there a second?" he asked.

Vinny stopped because he had no choice. The guy was right in front of him. Vinny recognized the accent from the pub the night before. Everything and everyone stood still as the man approached Jack's widow. "Mrs. Doyle, I'm here to tell you, in your loss of a husband, Ireland has lost a son, and many more will mourn than you will ever know."

Stepping back, he unzipped a bag he was carrying, shook out the green, orange and white Irish flag before carefully draping it over the coffin. From inside his jacket, he took out a beret and pair of black leather gloves, arranged them on the flag, and stepped back.

The waiting mourners were stunned. Vinny recognized the symbolism of what had been done. He smiled, just like the country Jack volunteered, for his body had been loved, fought over, stolen, and was now being laid to rest. Vinny wondered how long it would be before Ireland's journey would end, and it too could rest.

Jack's widow spoke out simply and clearly. "Let's bury him."

The End.

Ring of Fire

We were in the queue for our free dinner tickets—a daily ritual for most of us. Sammo was behind me.

"Going to The Parade?" he asked.

"Yeah, chip shop, then the park."

"We can go to our house if you like?" he said.

Sammo was my best mate, but I ignored the offer anyway.

"Vinny, do you fancy that? Going to ours."

What I fancied was Teresa Connor. If I could see her in The Parade, then fuck Sammo's.

"What about your dad?"

"He'll be out. Gets his giro today, so he'll be in the bookies."

"Alright, but let's go to the chippy first."

The queue didn't take long. Jack ticked off the names as he gave out the tickets. 'Mr Foreman or 'Jack' as we called him, also taught religious education. He was always called Jack. Teacher's names were passed down from one generation to the next. He was a hairy bastard and had hairs coming out of his knuckles, long black fuckers that poked out of his nose, even his ears. Maybe it was after Jack the Ripper. Or Jack and the Beanstalk. Those fucking hairs were thick enough for that. There was definitely something wrong with him.

We sat in The Parade, the geographic centre of Speke:

two rows of steel-shuttered shops with a grey paved square in between. Groups of youths positioned themselves around the square. Kids from the Catholic All Hallows wore uniforms. Those from Speke Comp didn't. This made it easier to work out who was whom.

The Parade was neutral during the day; at night, it became no man's land. I was holding out, waiting to see if Teresa would appear. There were a few girls from All Hallows among the lunchtime shoppers, but she wasn't with them. Teresa was from Eastern Avenue, so it was hard to see her at night. Everyone stayed in their part of the estate—to venture out was dangerous. I wanted to see her, but I didn't have the balls to go where she lived.

Sammo's younger brother Ricky came over.

"What the fuck do you want?" Sammo was never friendly to Ricky.

"Nothing, just seeing what you're doing."

"What does it look like we're doing, shithead?" Sammo reached out to clout him round the head, but Ricky was used to this and jumped back.

Sammo continued, "Fuck off. I've told you not to follow me around."

"So, you don't want some of this then?"

Ricky pulled a Mars bar out of his pocket. "Or this?" A Crunchie. "Or..." with a final flourish, he waved a Kit Kat, triumph shining on his face.

Sammo leapt at him, and this time managed to grab Ricky. "You fucker, have you been in me mam's purse again?"

Ricky ducked down and tried to pull away but was wrestled to the ground.

"Gerroff. I haven't touched her purse."

A passing shopper weighed down by heavy bags made an effort to intervene. "Let him up, you bully."

Sammo shouted back, "He's been robbing from me mam's purse."

The woman gave Ricky a dirty look, and before she walked on, she said, "Little bugger. Give him a slap from me."

Sammo carried on his interrogation. "Where'd you get the money for them?"

Ricky struggled with his brother's knee sticking in his chest.

"Hi, Vinny." Teresa smiled.

I hadn't noticed them approach. I was so wrapped up in Sammo's display. Teresa was with Marie, Sammo's sister. Teresa was gorgeous—soft blonde hair that fell to her shoulders and white, even teeth.

"You coming over to ours?" Marie asked.

"It was the frogs," said Ricky, still pinned to the floor.

"What about the fuckin frogs?" Sammo wouldn't give up his advantage.

I saw an opportunity to show my authority. "Leave him alone. Anyway, what's he on about frogs?"

"Look." Ricky got to his feet and gingerly slipped his hand into his blazer pocket. He pulled something out and, keeping his palm closed, advanced toward me.

"Look, you've killed it now." He pulled a face at his brother.

It was about an inch long, a real miniature frog. It would have been perfectly formed, but it was oozing a kind of yellow fluid over his hand and lay twitching. Ricky turned and threw it along the pavement. It splattered and bounced a few times before disappearing beneath the feet of shoppers. He wiped his hand on his blazer.

"Where'd you get that?" Although disgusted, I was also curious.

Sammo replied, "We've got a bucket full in our backyard."

Marie and Teresa had started walking off.

Shit. I watched them cross The Parade hoping Teresa would turn to look. "Come on then, let's make a move."

Sammo and Ricky fell in on either side of me. We passed the shops, shutters raised for the day. Leaving The Parade, we walked through the streets of large, red-brick council houses with gardens hedged by privets.

Ricky sensed his acceptance and talked on. "I got a load of spawn from a pond near the airport. We've had them for a few weeks now. They turn into tadpoles first, then like a half frog, half tadpole, and this week into proper little frogs.

"Okay, David fuckin Attenborough. What I want to know is, how did you get the sweets?"

Ricky beamed. "I sold three of the frogs in school this morning. I would've sold the other as well before it was squashed."

Their house was on the edge of Speke, separated from the factories beyond by a dual carriageway that formed a ring around the estate. The front gardens were smaller in these houses, with two-foot-high brick walls instead of the privet hedges in family houses. I could understand not being able to walk through any of the estates that surround us for fear of being caught and beaten; that was natural. But now Speke itself had split up into east, west, and central. Teresa lived in the eastern end, and I was fucked.

As soon as we got near the house, we could hear the music. The front windows were wide open, and 'Ben' by Micheal Jackson blared out. Sammo ran on ahead while Ricky strode along at my side.

"I'll kill that Marie. If me dad comes back, he'll go crazy If we're making so much noise." Sammo complained.

"Our Marie fancies you." Ricky volunteered.

"Shut the fuck up, Ricky."

Ricky changed tack. "Do you want some of the frogs? I don't mind. We've got loads."

Reaching the house, Ricky kicked open the little wooden gate and ran down the short path to the open front door. The music had been turned down, and the windows closed. The hallway was so small you could step right through it into the living room. Marie and Teresa were sitting on the settee, cigarettes pointedly raised in hands resting on crossed knees. They were laughing as I entered. Teresa stared straight at me.

Marie spoke first. "Hiya, Vinny."

"You ever get up to St Ambrose?" Teresa asked.

"Nah, I go to St Christopher's. You should come down sometime." I was being brave inviting her.

"They've got a disco at St Ambrose. There's one on Friday night. Marie's coming, aren't you?"

Marie smiled in agreement.

I was stuck. It was easy for girls; they could go anywhere within the estate.

"Yeah. Okay, that'll be great. I'll see you there then." I lied. I couldn't say anything else. I wouldn't go. It would be stupid, but I couldn't tell her that.

"Hey, Vinny," Sammo shouted. "Look, here they are."

Sammo and Ricky were in the backyard, just outside the kitchen door. Stepping out of the kitchen. I joined them round a black plastic bucket. It had a heavy piece of hardboard over the top. Ricky lifted the hardboard; the dirty brown water was bubbling with activity.

Marie and Teresa stood in the doorway. Teresa leaned forward to look. "Ergh, that's disgusting."

Ricky plunged his arm into the bucket and came up with a closed fist. "Shall I show him the trick?" He was looking anxiously at his brother.

"Yeah, go on." Sammo was laughing.

"You're sick." Marie pulled a face,

Ricky led the way into the greasy kitchen as Sammo took control. "You have to be careful. The little bastards jump all over the place."

Ricky held his fist above a ring on the cooker. Sammo ignited the gas and turned the flame low. This was Ricky's cue to lower his hand and place the frog in the centre of the ring. Sammo turned the flame up quickly. The frog sat in the centre of the ring. Untouched by the flame, its dark eyes stared out. As the flame grew, its body and legs began to twitch.

Sammo's face also twitched but with excitement. "Look,

it won't jump."

Marie pulled Teresa back into the living room. Before she left, our eyes met. They were a soft blue, not icy or hard, and there was something easy about them.

Meanwhile, the frog didn't jump. It sat still in the ring of fire, although its body convulsed. I don't know if it was trying to jump or this was just a reaction to the heat. Its skin began to darken and crack. Its big eyes shrank back, and still, it didn't jump. Finally, the twitching stopped, and the blackened body began to shrivel. The frog never jumped.

"Wait, it's not finished yet." Sammo urged Ricky on. "Go on."

"Is it done?" Ricky asked.

"Yeah, Kentucky fried." Sammo turned the gas off, and Ricky tossed the charred body between his hands.

"Here." Ricky pulled one of the legs off the frog's body, picked the skin away, and popped a slim piece of flesh into his mouth.

"Frog's legs." Sammo laughed.

I never did go out with Teresa, and for many years wondered if I would ever leave the estate. Eventually, I jumped.

The End

The Taxman

She ran up the stairs, her bare feet slapping the cold linoleum. As she neared the top, she could taste the oil from the paraffin heater on the empty landing. The doors to the three bedrooms and bathroom were open, allowing the warm breath of the paraffin to spread.

She didn't bother with the light but crossed quickly to her room, closing the door firmly behind her. She let her skirt drop and, in one movement, raised her jumper and blouse over her head. She slipped on the nightie. Between the cold cotton sheets in the darkened room, she was alone, her head pressed firmly into the pillow, a tear welled behind the closed lid as she waited…

**

The car turned the corner slowly. Joey knew no one walked these streets for pleasure, and those with purpose had long gone.

"Okay, pull in here a minute." Joey was in easy command. "Paul, jump out, go the corner, have a look down the street, then come back."

Paul eased open the car door and climbed from the back of the vehicle. He left the door open just an inch and walked off. They saw him approach the corner. Darkness was never complete here—the faint orange glow of the streetlamps with the diffused light through curtains meant darkness, physical darkness, was never total.

"I don't want any fucking messing about in there. You understand?"

Jonno and Mike nodded. "No problems, Joe, just in and out."

Paul made his way back to the car. "It's okay, Joe. No one there."

Joe nodded to Mike. "Ring him."

Mike's thin, drawn face topped by bleached blonde hair was sweating. He lit a cigarette and placed it between his chapped lips. When he exhaled, the smoke poured between his cracked and broken teeth. Mike snapped open his phone, recalled a number from memory, and waited.

"Yo."

"Who's this?"

"I need some gear."

"Fuck off." The harsh voice filled the car.

"No, it's me, Mikey...Come on...Fuck...you know me... come on, it's sound..."

"Where are you?"

"Just on my way now...take it easy...I had a result today."

"Cash...no fucking shit."

"Yeah, cash...like I said, I had a result."

"Who's with you?"

"Just a cab...am in the cab now...be there in five."

The line went dead.

Joe looked at Jonno. "C'mon, let's do it."

Jonno slipped the car into gear, and they moved off, slowing to round a corner. They entered a wide street, straight as a die both ways. There was no other traffic on the road. They pulled up outside a terraced house in the middle of a row. The only difference between it and its neighbour was the wrought iron gate fixed to the brickwork surrounding the heavy wooden door.

Mike got out the back. Jonno and Paul ran up each side of the path and stood out of sight on either side of the iron gate. Mike walked slowly up to the door and rang the bell. Sweating and dishevelled, Mike didn't need to act a part. A hatch opened in the door.

"Hey, fuckhead," a voice rang out. "Haven't seen you in a while…thought you'd fucked up."

Mikey grinned. "Nah…just scoring shit…but had a good day…time for some real shit."

"Long as you got what it takes…"

"Yeah." Mikey pulled a wedge of cash from his pocket.

"Nice one. What you want then?"

"I wanna see Gray…"

"What for?"

"Business." Mikey waved the wedge in front of the hatch.

"Hold on."

The hatch slammed shut. Mikey glanced nervously at Paul and Jonno on either side of him. The locks on the door were turned. They could hear the metal scrape as a bar was removed. The front door opened, and a latch was released to open the iron gate. The gate opened slowly, creaking on its hinges. Mikey stepped forward but was pulled aside by Paul with one hand while his other hand brought down the weight of the firearm he was holding on the skull of the man behind the door. Blood spurted over the wallpaper in the hallway. Pushed aside by Paul, all the man could do was stare at the red constellation that spread over the wall. Paul and Jonno were both through the door and inside the living room of the house in seconds. Guns drawn, and arms extended, they waved the barrels at the figures in the room, shouting, "Don't move...Don't fucking move!" The trembling hands holding lethal weapons were enough for the occupants. They sat stock still, eyes wide with fright.

The three men and one woman in the room sat around a glass-topped coffee table. Joe entered calmly. He strode between Paul and Jonno. The woman began to get up. She was in her early twenties, slim with short dark hair. Joe couldn't help but notice she was pretty, very pretty, with wide dark eyes and a fine, fragile nose. As she rose, he swung round in a pirouette, the circular movement increasing the power of the kick that landed in her face. The force of it sent her sprawling backwards into the settee. Her cry was stifled by shock. She slumped back, blood pouring from her broken nose, her hands feeling for shape.

"Did I say she could get up? No, I fucking didn't...the money...now." Joe was looking at the occupant of the armchair that faced the glass coffee table.

"Danny, get him the fucking money."

One of the men on the settee already spattered with the woman's blood looked at Joe.

Joe nodded, "Paul go with him."

They were back inside a minute. No one in the living

room had moved or spoken. The woman on the settee lay moaning. Danny returned to his place.

Joe moved across the room until he stood beside the man in the armchair. "The money good?"

Paul looked inside the large blue cotton bag he was carrying. "Fuck yeah."

Joe placed his hand behind the head of the man in the armchair, forcing him down to the table. His sweating face smeared the glass. Joe looked around. Frightened faces stared back. He held the moment, then raised his hand, and before the guy could move his head, Joe had formed a fist and brought it crashing down on the back of the man's head. The glass smashed. Before the cries had finished leaving the man's mouth, Joe was on his way home to Marie.

***

Jenny walked straight up to the bar, the bandage a shocking white against her discoloured face. Heads turned, looked furtively, and then moved away as she flashed her bruised eyes round the pub. The landlady, Karen, a slight woman in her mid-thirties with shoulder-length blonde hair and wearing a navy-blue trouser suit, walked up to meet Jenny.

"Bacardi Breezer." Pulling a ten-pound note from the pocket of her full-length leather coat, Jenny continued. "Aren't you going to ask?"

Karen placed the drink on the bar. "None of my business, love."

"If it's none of your business, what's that bitch doing here?" Jenny nodded down the bar toward Marie.

Marie stood with a newspaper spread out on the bar in front of her. She looked up but didn't move.

Karen answered. "I meant it." She slammed Jenny's change on the bar. "It's none of my business, and this is my pub."

Marie turned the page of her newspaper. She tried to focus on the type, but the blue-black bruising and the white bandage clung to her peripheral vision.

"Nice fella, eh, Marie?" Jenny was walking down the length of the bar.

Karen caught up with her. "Look, I've told you. You're welcome to your drink, but that's all…if you've got anything to sort out, you do it outside." She placed herself between Jenny and Marie.

"Oh, it'll be sorted. Don't you worry about that." Jenny took a long drink from her bottle and placed it back on the bar. "Just thought you'd like to see." She raised her voice and turned round, displaying herself to the other drinkers. "Big hard man, Joey Delaney. Well, take a good look, 'cos this is what the shithouse did to me." She turned toward Marie, but Karen blocked her way and stood with her arms folded.

"Okay. That's it." Karen unfurled her arms and swept Jenny toward the door. "You were warned. Now, that's it. Out."

Jenny put her bottle on a table on the way out. Holding the door open, she turned back toward Marie. "You just tell him, he got the wrong people this time. Tell that shithouse, he's fucked."

Karen walked across to Marie. "For fuck's sake, Marie,

was that Joe?"

Marie looked straight back at her, "I don't know, and to be honest, I don't care. She's a slag, and whatever she got, she had coming."

Karen shrugged. "Okay, but come on…"

She wasn't allowed to finish. "No, leave it, Karen. I don't want to hear. You're a mate, but that's it, okay?"

Karen raised her hands. "Like I said, none of my business."

Marie went back to her newspaper and tried to focus on the words. She was conscious of the eyes staring at her. She folded the paper away and went to serve.

Marie walked quickly through the estate. In the nether world of a winter afternoon, between light and dark, she hurried toward their home. She slowed, only when she realised Joe wasn't there. The car was missing, and the lights were off.

Closing the door and kicking off her shoes, she felt the warmth of the soft carpet beneath her feet. A burst of light responded to a flicked switch. She pressed a button on the remote, and the sound of Sinead O'Connor filled the flat. The doors to the bedroom and bathroom were open. Everywhere she looked, she could see Joe—the open door of the wardrobe where his suits hung waiting for use, a bathrobe lifeless without him laying collapsed on the floor.

She walked into their bedroom and let her skirt fall, and lifted her jumper over her head. In bra and pants, she moved toward the dressing table. Closing in on her reflection, she picked up her face cream. It no longer hurt, to look. She needed the cream to tighten her skin, to close the open pores.

It was while smoothing the cream down the side of her nose that Jenny's face appeared. It was the colour she couldn't forget—such a strange mix of purple and blue shot through with fine strands of red. Marie worked the cream into her skin, rubbing the excess into her hands. *Fuck Jenny.*

She slipped into bed and lying between the smooth cold sheets. She thought of the time before, in a clinical way now, no tears, no fear. She remembered the feeling of helplessness, like a doll manipulated, moved this way and that, touched, probed. Then the shame and guilt, feeling dirty, the clammy sweat of her flesh, unreal. Like a cold day remembered in the summer warmth, it was a different world. She was rebuilding. Was this it? The end of her journey? She didn't know. She didn't want children…no. She didn't want the power, the responsibility. She would live and die, and her memories would die with her like soiled, used goods.

Marie was woken a few hours later. She felt his touch before she heard his voice. Joey had reached out to touch her cool skin, running the back of his finger down her upper arm. He sat on the bed next to her, his weight making her lean into him. She woke slowly, enjoying his touch.

"Hi, babe."

She didn't move. She didn't want his hand to stop. It was in these touches, the gentle stroke and communion of skin, that she found his humanity. He kicked off his shoes and sat on the bed, leaning back against the wall. Marie was pulling back the cover to draw him in when his phone rang.

"Yeah."

"I think we've got a problem." Jonno sounded nervous.

"What are you on about?"

"The shit the other night."

"The tax?"

"Yeah."

"Come on, then, spit it out."

"It was Harry Kane's gear. That fucker was just laying it out."

"Who did you speak to?"

"I got a call this morning."

"Okay, don't panic. I'll sort it out. You just bring the cash round."

His voice was always controlled. His words carried no warmth. Communication was not for expression but to precipitate an action, thoughts remaining intangible and inaccessible.

Marie knew the phone call wasn't good. "Will you be back tonight?"

He stood and walked to the doorway. "Yeah, should be."

Marie sought his eyes. Of the softest blue, they spoke no language. They were a warm gaze and a cold stare existing at once and together, neither seen without the presence of the other, their coexistence, as baffling to Marie as the tenderness she found in a man without remorse or pity.

Marie heard the door close, then the thud of car doors and the muffled growl of the engine. He was off into the night.

Seated in the back of the car, Joe gave the instructions. "Pick up Jonno, then we'll go and see Charlie." They drove around the estate, the silver-grey Jaguar XJ6 commanding the narrow streets. After collecting Jonno, they drove on for a few minutes. Their world was small. The car stopped in the lay by to a row of shops. Heavy steel shutters protected the shop windows. Graffiti was spreading, flowing down from the walls and shutters. It crept out over the cracked pavement. A yellow 'Taxi' sign was fixed over a shopfront. Its windows were boarded with only the dark red doorway exposed.

Joe led the way through. He received a nod from a man who was standing at the bottom of a narrow staircase. An old carpet covered the stairs, its floral pattern matching the wallpaper. At the top of the stairs, Joe faced three doors. Joe took Paul's blue cloth bag and entered the first door on the left. Paul and Jonno waited on the landing. A large window allowed light to flood the room, broken only by the vertical shadows of the bars outside it. Charlie was seated behind an old battered desk. To his right in an armchair and cradling a cup of coffee was a second man.

Charlie didn't rise but shifted his weight behind the desk as if in greeting. "Joey, boy, nice to see you…heard you've been busy."

Joe looked at the swollen face behind the desk. Its features were shapeless. The thin lips of his mouth sat in the midst of fleshy corpulence. Joe lowered himself into an empty chair in front of the desk.

"Seven and a half," Joe said, placing the cotton bag on the desk.

The man to Charlie's right picked up the bag. He emptied its contents on a small side table and began counting.

Joe placed an envelope on the desk. "It needs to go back to Harry. This is for the inconvenience."

Joe leaned forward in his chair. "Tell Harry we got the wrong information. We wouldn't have gone near if we knew."

Charlie smiled, "They won't let this go, you know that?"

Joe was quick to reply. "Look, he's got more than his cash, back. We don't want any problems."

"You're not listening, Joe. He won't let this go. Something about an eye for an eye."

Joe stood. "Come on, Charlie, there's no need for that."

"I'm just passing on the message, Joe."

"It's business, Charlie; mistakes get made."

The smile reappeared, and the thin lips stretched momentarily. "And debts have to be paid."

***

Marie had given up expecting the warmth of normal companionship, shared ideals, or the knowledge of secrets and desires that bind many lovers. Theirs was a world of physical sensations. No one else had been able to make her feel every inch of skin, to know and understand her body, the life that existed in touch alone. When she slept naked next to him, she could feel his passion, his concern. His flesh spoke to her in a way she understood, and her own responded. In animal warmth, she knew Joe—in physical senses, nothing unreal or wished for, nothing outside the moment—in touch alone, no promises, no expectations, and yet it was more, the slightest brush of his lips over her body, the longing poured through an embrace. These were the testament of their shared life.

***

Marie dressed slowly as Joe slipped back into a light sleep. Her nakedness was a release, allowing the spirit enlivened by Joe to walk freely. She felt strange, unused to the liberation of a body mortified in times gone by. She could look at her own transition now, could retrace the halting steps of recovery. The memory of her shock that first night when Joe did no more than hold her when she had tensed at the expected invasion. Her confusion as she lay beside him contained a fear of rejection. Alive with anticipation, she felt every movement as a preliminary to the inevitable consummation. She slept that night, as deep and profound a sleep as she had known. No dreams, no nightmares, and her waking brought with it a sense of balance, of order, that somehow her life was being reshaped. Something had shifted. It took a while to realise, but slowly she did as the warmth from Joe had begun to eat away at the darkness within her. She never again felt as fundamental a change as that first night, but it had continued. She had changed. Something from him had changed her, allowed her to live in the body she once thought was dead.

Joe was awake. "Are you working again?"

"Yeah, but just the afternoon."

"Why? You don't need the money."

"It gets me out."

"It's a dive, a shithole."

"Go back to sleep."

When he woke again, she was gone. Daylight was streaming through the thin half-closed curtains. In the disordered room, he could feel her presence, the sweet smell of perfume hung in the air around him. Beneath this, he determined the faint but real odour of Marie. He closed his eyes and tried to capture the essence of Marie, but nothing came. He was awake, and with wakefulness came reality, and with reality, the cries of the night before. He didn't feel guilt or shame, nor did he remember to enjoy or relive. The cries of the last night mingled with those of earlier, and those yet to come. They were an unceasing companion stretching out beyond him. The cries of the night before bore no identity or brought no image but merged into a single wretched cry that had been ever-present in his life. He raised himself, separated now from the experience of Marie. He walked among her things as so much detritus and encumbrance. Fumbling through a jacket, he found his phone.

"Jonno, go sit outside the pub."

"Marie's?"

"Yeah, when Charlie's boys go in, don't do anything, just call me. Okay?"

"What's going on, Joe?"

"Time to pay the debt."

"Marie?"

"Yeah...an eye for an eye. On second thoughts, as soon as you see them go in, call an ambulance for her. Then ring me."

The End

Walkways in The Sky

Lips pursed, Harry blew out the trumpet sound of the Last Post. The wail of his voice was in mockery, not respect. The funeral was real, the death was real. In the Allerton Cemetery grounds, the trumpet and tears were real. In the act of grieving for one of their own, uniformed boys became men. In the act of grieving their own, parents and siblings became less.

Buuur Burrr Harry re-enacted the Last Post and trumpeted to his wife's tears.

"How can you be so cruel?" Karen asked.

But she knew the answer. Surrounded by uniformed youth in the company of real men, Harry was diminished. He knew it, and she knew it. His bravado and cruelty were in a place of strength.

"It's not fair," said Macca watching as his sister cried. He feared what was coming but didn't know how to stop it.

"Those fucking bastards. They are nothing. Did you see them strutting around in their uniforms? I could have had any of them one to one. The hardest in Halewood I was, no one messed with our family."

They were not in Halewood, where he was from. They were not in Speke, where Karen was from. They were in Netherley, where people lived, but no one was from, built on the Eastern edge of Liverpool. That was how they lived—on the edge: a planner's paradise and a tenant's nightmare. Tomorrow's living today—prefabricated concrete panels in a new system of construction. Living by design, thousands of people moved out of the city centre in slum clearances, now trapped in damp-ridden, vermin-infested concrete boxes, four or five storeys high, high-level walkways, and connecting bridges between blocks.

When the first slap hit Karen, she stifled her cries. Macca knew she was trying to hide her pain and fear, but nothing could hide the anger and cruelty in Harry.

"Leave her alone," Macca pleaded, too scared to shout or demand.

"Shut up, or you'll get it as well."

"Go in the bedroom, look after Sharon," said Karen.

Sharon was Macca's niece, barely walking, and sleeping now. Macca knew Karen was sending him away to protect him.

Harry stood and crossed the room. He leaned over Karen, who curled into a ball. Macca knew what was coming. Karen cried in fear.

"All of them, I could have had all of them," Harry boomed in anger.

Macca said, "Karen, I'm going to phone mum."

Karen looked up and shouted, "No!"

Harry punched. Macca saw it hit. He felt the blow on his sister's face. The tears poured from his eyes. Tears of anger and frustration. *I'm phoning.* He choked and fled.

He ran through the concrete walkways, his feet pounding out his hatred. *A phone, a phone.* He ran through the tunnelled high-level connecting bridges, down the rancid urine-stained staircase, across the shit covered grass. He found a phone, but he had no money to phone, and his mum had no phone to answer. He stood and cried as he waited. *How long do we wait till we know it's over? When do we admit dreams have turned to dust?*

Built in 1968, new technology for a new age, demolished fifteen years later. The planners awarded and moved on. The technology of tomorrow, creative futures for, but not by or of, the people. Karen and Harry divorced. Macca and Sharon grew. Everyone was battered and bruised by walkways in the sky.

The End

Born Again

The voice reached in pulling me out.

"Can you hear me? Anthony, I need you to wake up."

I could see colours and shapes floating in and out of focus, moving in waves. This wasn't physical. I knew my eyes were closed. It was my brain trying to focus. After a while, things became clearer. 'I think. Therefore, I am' was not for me. My brain was engaged in a struggle for life. 'I am. Therefore, I can think.' Allowing the consciousness of thought. I knew that I was, but where I was, who I was, I did not know.

He was there whenever I was conscious, which meant he must have been there constantly. Every time I managed to surface, he was there.

"Good Morning Anthony, and how are you feeling today? Come on now, you can do it. Come on, back to the land of the living."

I didn't know him, I was sure of that. Yet his voice seemed familiar. Before I could open my eyes or recognise sound as speech, his sound had been echoing around inside my head. I wasn't sure if I was hearing, remembering or imagining it. Each time I surfaced, I grew stronger, and so did the voice.

"Are you with us yet, mate?"

When speech came, it was weak and forced. "Who are you?"

"Never mind that now. What's important is that you are with us again. And not before time, if you don't mind me saying."

"How long have I been here?"

"Erhh, looking at your chart, I'd say too long, much too long. You've got to get your shit together. Can't be lying around in bed all day. By the way, car accident it was."

"What?"

"Well, I know, at some point, you are going to ask. 'How did I get here,' so I just thought I would short circuit it, tell you now before you ask. And while I'm in the mood to dispense information, you're forty-three and by all accounts a bit of a tosser. Not good my friend. Not good at all."

"What? Who are you? Are you a doctor?"

"Nah, although I did consider it once, but far too much studying for me."

"Then what are you doing here?"

"Now, look, don't go getting all wound up. I've been sort of assigned to look after you. So lie back and relax."

"Wait a minute, you said I was forty-three."

"Yeah, that's right."

"How do you know?"

"It's all here on your chart, and anyway, I know you pretty well. Or at least I used to."

"Then tell me, what's going on?"

"No, you don't get me that easy. I can't go filling your head with facts and information like there's no tomorrow. I mean, who knows what would happen?"

"But I need to know, want to know. Who am I? What

am I?"

"Ahh yeah, but you see if I told you, then you would become the person I said you were."

"What's wrong with that? If it's who I am."

"But you don't know that do you? I could say you are a really smart city trader, with a Porsche down there in the car park and an apartment overlooking the river—that you are rich and successful, and before you know it, lo and behold, that's who you'd be. You'd be barking out orders to me like the hired help, sending out for espressos while on the phone to your Harley Street doctor. No, no."

"Is that who I am?"

"No, that's just the point, but who's to say if I told you that's who you were you wouldn't become him? But if you were him, I'd certainly make sure you had no tomorrows. That's the problem, don't you see? You do see, don't you? Oh no, don't go now. Are you slipping off into that little wonderland of yours? Anthony, stay with me, mate, don't go yet. It's just getting interesting."

The problem with darkness is that you don't know what's in it and how deep or how long it is. The parameters of the known world disappear, and we become lost in time and space, in the realm of the unknown. It was from here that I would have to claw my way back into the light, each time searching for something recognisable, something I could focus on—anything from which to draw strength. My awakenings were bittersweet. Each time, I realised I knew more than before, but each time knowing there was so much more I didn't know.

"I have children."

"Let me see, yeah, here we go, two kids. Not bad mate, you're getting the hang of this. Just out of curiosity, how did you know?"

"It's something you wouldn't understand.

How old are you? Nineteen, twenty? What do you know about anything?"

"I'm twenty-three actually, and by this age, Alexander had conquered half the world, Mozart had written his best work, Trotsky was head of the St Petersburg Soviet, and Shakespeare had written his first play. So, you mind your manners, old man. I might just have something you want."

"The only thing I want from you is information. How did I know about the children? I just know, like I know outside this room, the sun rises and sets every day. Even though I can't see it, I know grass is green, and the sky is blue. I know because, like that knowledge, my children are a part of me. Whoever that is. And whoever you are, I know you have nothing to do with this hospital."

"Yes, yes, very lyrical. I suppose a dose of mortality does that to people."

"Who are you? What do you want?"

"Just hold on there, big boy. You haven't earned the right yet. I am Tony, by the way. Okay, now, where was I? Oh yeah, you've got two kids. Boy and a girl as it happens, but they haven't been in here to see you have they, eh? Don't you find that odd? No one here, just little old Tony. Truth is, mate, no one cares if you live or die. Not even your own family, never mind humanity at large. It wouldn't notice if you never set foot outside this place again. Just think on that for a while, and maybe you'll have a little more humility. Less of this wanting-answers-on-demand."

"You bastard."

"Not me, no. See if I was the bastard, it would be me lying in that bed with no one caring if I lived or died, and it's not is it? It's you. So what brought you to this sorry state, eh? You want to know? Do you?"

"Of course, I do."

"Well, let's see then. A failed father, a failed marriage, oh, and look at this, a failed career. Not much of a life is it?"

"How do I know you're telling the truth?"

"Was I right about the kids?"

"Yes, you know you were."

"Well then, you just listen up. If there's one thing I can guarantee, it's that you'll get the truth from me. In fact, I'm the only person who cares enough to give it to you straight. You see, we've got a debt to settle, and right now, I'm in the mood to take payment."

"Why are you doing this? What debt?"

"I want my future back. I want my life. I want to know what happened to my ambitions, my dreams. But first I need you to understand yourself. Are you ready for that?"

"Yes."

"Okay, where was I? Divorced, don't see much of the kids, just about on speaking terms with the ex-wife. Live in a one-bedroom flat, and worst of all, a bloody salesman. Is that enough to stimulate the grey matter? Why don't you cogitate on that for a while, then we'll see where you are when the world lets you back in."

"I'm fine. I'm not tired. Carry on."

"No, it's time for bo-bo's mate. Have a kip, take a rest. I want you fully functioning so you can explain the miserable waste of your life, and I only get that when you start putting the pieces together. You see it really is true: I only know what you know. I see what you see, but that doesn't mean we will agree on what we are seeing. So off you go mate and recover a bit more of my future."

His voice followed me into the darkness. I knew he was telling the truth. Earlier knowledge had risen from the depths to gently break the surface. It now surged in great waves that crashed within me. The aching pain that announced my children, the knowledge that my life was not theirs, that they cried, smiled, and lived in another place with other people. The contempt, their mother, my ex-wife bore for me.

His word 'failure' covered everything. Was he right? Is this who I was? All I was? These waves were living links that tied me to the world outside this room, a world in which I would fight for my place to belong. I had made mistakes, but my life was worth living. With this knowledge came confidence and clarity. It was true I was divorced, but I loved my kids, and no one was going to stop me from seeing them again. I didn't know who this Tony was, but he had no right to do this. This time would be different. I would not be bullied or intimidated. Whatever the hell was going on, it was about to stop.

"So, you're still here?"

"Large as life."

"Look, I don't know what your game is, but I've had enough. Nurse, Nurse, Doctor!"

"You can shout all you like, no one will hear you, It's just you and me. You'd better listen to me and listen good. If you ever want to get out of this place, you need to convince me that you deserve to live. I have the power of life and death over you. Your life is in my hands, and I don't mind telling you, at this moment, the balance is not in your favour."

"What? This can't be happening. Who the hell are you?"

"Have you never looked in a mirror? Less worn out and bedraggled, I admit, but it's there. Don't you recognise yourself? The cleaner, sharper, younger you?"

"Are you crazy?"

"Time to get on with things."

"What things?"

"Working out what you have done with my life, whether you deserve the right to live it."

"What kind of statement is that? I know what I've done with my life: I've lived it. That's what it is for, isn't it? I'm not responsible for you, whoever you are."

"I'm afraid that's exactly where you are wrong, mate. You see, I am, or was you, the real deal, not the washed-out version in front of us."

"This is stupid. If you are me, then how can you kill me? How do you have this power of life and death? That would be killing yourself, suicide."

"No, that's the point: I'm already dead. The person I was, you were, twenty years ago, doesn't exist anymore. The things I believed in and cared about have been betrayed.

Everything I considered important, you have managed to destroy. In fact, everything I was is now so thoroughly corrupted that killing you now would be like putting a dog out of its misery. A mercy killing."

"I don't have to justify myself to you or anyone else."

"That's not what you used to say. Remember this?"

***

The chair was speaking from a raised platform at the front of the hall. The room was hot and stuffy. Murmured voices lent a constant vibration to the air.

"Order, order, please." He looked across at the speaker who was returning to his chair also on the platform. "I'm sure you will all join me in thanking our colleague from the National Union of Mineworkers for his rousing appeal for moral and financial support in their struggle to defend jobs. All that remains is for me to remind you that we will be collecting for the Miners Hardship Fund."

He raised his eyes to the back of the room. "Tony, Tony, where are the buckets?"

"They are here, by the door. We'll collect from people on the way out."

The chair continued, "Right, thank you. Please, give generously. I would also like to thank the committee of the University Labour Club for organising this meeting."

The hundred or so students packed into the room began moving at once. Tony shook and rattled the bucket as people pressed through the doorway.

"Here, Kate." Tony gave her a spare bucket, and she

took it to the opposite side of the doorway, doubling their capacity to reach people.

Coins flowed into the buckets. People queued and waited to make sure they could make their contribution.

"Are you coming to the pub?" Mike asked.

"Sure, let me finish up here," Tony answered.

As the crowd thinned out, Kate joined Tony. "Great meeting."

"Yeah, I know, fantastic, wasn't it?"

"Here." Kate handed her bucket over. "I'll get you a pint."

"Thanks." The eye contact was just a little longer than necessary, making Tony smile when Kate had left.

***

Later, Tony made his way through the crowded bar. Music and voices combined to create a buzz of energy.

"Over here." Kate waved him over to the table. "I saved you a seat, and here's your pint."

"What's this? Favouritism?" asked Mike.

"Don't be silly. He was helping out," said Kate.

Tony smiled and accepted the seat. He took a large drink from his beer. "That tastes good."

"How much did they collect?" asked Kate.

"I don't know. They were still counting it as I left, but it looked good."

"Good speaker, though, wasn't he?" Kate said.

"Good looking, you mean?" said Mike.

"You're so cynical. Six months on strike is a long time,"

Kate replied.

"She's right, not everything is a joke," said Tony.

"Lighten up, for Christ's sake," Mike said.

"Look over there, that's him, isn't it?" Kate pointed across the bar.

"Yeah, with the tosser from the Labour Party, who chaired the meeting," said Mike.

Kate rose from her seat. "I'm going to invite them over."

"I told you she fancied him," said Mike.

"Behave, will you? They're coming over. No snarky comments, okay?"

Charlie, the miner, was first to reach the table. Mike and Tony stood to shake hands.

"Good to meet you. You spoke really well," Tony said.

"Thanks, but I've got to admit, I've had a lot of practise recently."

They were joined at the table by Kate and the chair of the meeting.

"What did you think of the meeting?" Tony asked.

"It was good. It was great to see so many young people there."

"Well, you've got Tony to thank for that. He spent his days this week putting posters and flyers all over the place," said Kate.

"The Labour Party has been collecting food every week outside the supermarkets," the chair added.

"Great strategy. We'll defeat Thatcher with tins of beans. It might be better if your leader knew what side he was on," said Mike.

"We're grateful for all the support we get, and believe it or not, the tins of beans come really handy when you've got kids to feed."

"If you're okay here for a minute, there's someone I should really go and speak to," said the chair.

"Yeah, of course," said Charlie.

"Yeah, you go and network, mate. Doesn't it drive you mad, people like him using the strike to try and climb the greasy pole?" Mike asked when the chair moved out of ear-shot.

"No, you get used to it. Everyone's got an agenda. At least we know what his agenda is, and right now, he's helping," said Charlie.

"The Labour Party has let you down, though. The leadership have been criticising you," said Mike.

"But there are thousands of ordinary members out there working to help the strike," said Kate.

"You're both right. There's no question if the Labour Movement had a leadership as committed to our class as Thatcher is to hers, this strike would have been over by now," said Charlie.

"Look, don't get me wrong, I'm on your side, but it's just a strike," said Mike.

"That may well be true, but who wins or loses this thing will determine politics in the UK for years, maybe even decades to come," said Charlie.

He rose from his seat. "It was really nice to meet you guys. Thanks again for the help in organising the meeting. I should find my people and make a move."

"No problem, and thank you," Tony said.

"Keep up the good fight, eh," said Mike.

Charlie moved away from the table and disappeared among the drinkers.

"You can be a right pain sometimes," Tony said to Mike.

"What? Just because I didn't fall at his feet?"

"No, because you think you are so bloody clever," said Kate.

"Oh, forgive me for not being Che Guevara. You two are the ones playing at politics, student radicals. At least I am honest," said Mike.

"The world is changing around us, not just this strike, but look at Nicaragua, Iran—real revolutions. All your cynicism does is show you are scared. You can't keep up, so sit on the sideline sniping," said Tony.

"Oh, right, and I suppose you're at the centre of this worldwide revolutionary movement, are you?" said Mike.

"Laugh all you like. I want my life to make a difference, to mean something," Tony replied.

"Well said," Kate agreed.

"It's about more than ourselves. The whole system needs changing," said Tony

"And who's going to change it? You?" asked Mike.

"Someone has to. Why not me?" answered Tony.

***

"I couldn't put it better myself, you see. You, or should I say,

I, started out so well. How did you mess it up?" Tony said.

"How can you do that? That was my life. How can you bring it back like that?" Anthony asked.

"Correction: that was my life. My life before you destroyed it."

"Am I crazy? Is that what's happening here? Who are you? You claim to be me, but you are stuck in some kind of time warp in the miners' strike in 1984."

"I represent the best in you. That's who I am. The best that you were and could have been. Engaged, committed, thinking about society, thinking beyond your own needs and ambitions. If my life meant anything, it was to reject the 'I'm-alright-Jack philosophy, reject the flag-waving and jingoism. I was part of the world, not just little England. So what happened? Come on, tell me. I need to know."

"Life is what happened. Jesus, no wonder I left you behind. You belong back then. If I have to argue with who I used to be, then so be it. If this is what it takes, I will get through this. You know something, who or whatever you are? You're right if you are me, or you are what I was then—you are dead. And do you know something else? I'm bloody glad you are."

"Okay. Got that out of your system? Perhaps we can move on then because this isn't about what you want—it's about what you have become. What you have turned me into. It makes me sick to even look at you."

"Don't get high and mighty with me because I remember you as well, and I'm not taking lectures off a po-faced git like you. I was lucky Kate took me back. Jesus, what a bleeding prat I was, you know, seeing you now, if that's who you are. I am well and truly glad to see the back of you."

"Driving round the country selling sweets? Is that what I'm reduced to? You'd better start coming up with something good because I am telling you, I won't end up as an embarrassment."

"Embarrassment? Don't get me started. You remember Tina, do you? Sexy, sophisticated, intelligent, and a real thinker, and what happened?"

"I didn't know her housemate parked in the drive."

"All the housemates, grabbing breakfast before rushing off to their high-powered jobs, and what happened? Tina's housemate goes out to her car, then comes back in holding a used condom in a tissue in her hand, complaining some low-life had stuck it on her windscreen wiper and spread the sperm all over her windscreen."

"The toilet wouldn't flush. What was I supposed to do?"

"Throwing a used condom out of the window, who would credit it?"

"Tina wasn't right for me, anyway."

"Not after that, she wasn't. Talk about red faces. Do you know what she is doing now? Do you? She is only one of the leading civil rights barristers in England, that's all."

"Okay, enough. Remember the darkness, do you? The place where your kids don't exist? Where nothing exists, where you simply disappear? Well, think on it, because I can send you back there, and believe me. I will."

I began to slip. I was sinking. Everything was slowing down. I couldn't feel my heartbeat. The light began to fade.

"No…No…wait…please…wait…"

"Okay, I hope you realise now how serious this is."

"Yes, yes, I do."

"Good, then maybe you can explain what happened to turn a class fighter into...well…into you."

"Class fighter? Come on, selling newspapers and going on a few demonstrations hardly makes you a working-class hero. Be fair. I mean, we weren't exactly dragged up in the backstreets of some council estate, were we?"

"It's not about where you come from, but what you do. Capitalism can only ever work for a minority. The bankers and industrialists will always be alright. The system has to exploit to survive—to be winners, there must be losers."

"Okay, look, I've heard the speeches—save it. You want to know what happened? I'll tell you, but there is no road to Damascus, no shining light. It didn't happen overnight. After the miner's strike, there was a feeling, well, if the miners can't win, who can? I know. I know it's narrow-minded and defeatist, but it was real. And it is also true that things were still happening around the world. In Ireland or South Africa, people were struggling. But nothing was happening here."

"So the Miners were defeated, and you thought 'there goes any chance of making the world a better place?' You gave up?"

"No, not like that. It wasn't as simple as that."

"Yes, it is. I can see it. You begin to make little compromises with life. You become just another individual whose only thought is me, me, me. How do I get through this? What job can I get? Where am I going to live? If that is not defeat, then I don't know what is."

"No, you are wrong. It wasn't *how do I get through this*."

***

The baby's heart monitor issued a regular beat.

"Arrgghh."

"Come on, love, you're doing fine," Anthony said.

Kate was leaning back, knees up, legs spread. "I'm not doing fine. Jesus, how much more of this?"

"You're dilated four centimetres. We need quite a bit more before we can do anything," the midwife said.

"It's been hours," Kate complained.

"Try walking around. It helps the baby."

"Walk? Are you kidding? I can't even stand up with all these tubes in me."

"I'll take those out. The baby is doing fine. We just need the baby to turn. We can reattach these when you are further along."

"What about the blood?" Anthony asked.

"It was the mucus plug. It's completely normal."

The midwife left the room.

"Come on, love, give me your arm. Let's try and walk."

Kate grunted as she climbed off the bed and paced unsteadily around the small room.

"Is that any better?"

"I just want it to be over. Why can't they give me something?"

"You've had the pethidine. She said, that's all for now."

"It's not bloody working."

"Come on, keep walking, it'll get better."

"That's easy for you to say."

"I'm sorry, really. I just don't know what to do," Anthony apologised.

"Don't worry, you are doing fine." Kate squeezed his hand.

"But I'm not, though, am I? You need someone who can look after both of you."

"Not now, eh?" Kate said.

"I mean it, I won't let you down. I promise."

***

The heart monitor's beeps increased and decreased in frequency.

"What's wrong?" asked Kate.

"I just want to take a look," said the doctor.

"What's happening? Why is it taking so long?" asked Anthony.

"Nicely dilated, looks about ten centimetres, that's fine, fully effaced might be O.P.," said the doctor.

"O.P. What's O.P.?" asked Anthony.

"Occipito-Posterior. The baby hasn't fully turned. Everything is ready, contractions,

dilation, but the baby won't come out in this position," said the midwife.

"We need to walk her again," said the doctor.

"I'm scared," Kate said.

"There's no need to be. Gravity and a little movement

can do the trick," said the midwife.

"What if it doesn't?" asked Anthony.

"Everything is fine. Depending on the baby's position, we have to be ready for the

forceps or ventouse, an episiotomy or a caesarean, but at the moment, these are all possibilities, and all these procedures are completely routine," said the doctor.

Kate began to cry.

"Don't worry, it'll be fine," said Anthony.

"How is it fine? They're going to drag the baby out of me. Can I have an epidural?"

"I wouldn't advise it. We need you to be able to bear down," the doctor answered.

"It will be alright," said Anthony.

"I'm sick of hearing that. It's not okay. Look at me. How is this okay?"

"Come on, then. Let's get you up," the midwife said.

"Call me if there's a change," said the doctor as he left.

Kate struggled to her feet. The movement prompted a cry of pain. "I think it's coming," she said.

"Here, grab my hand," said Anthony.

Kate walked up and down, round and round for a few minutes then Anthony helped her back onto the bed.

"The baby's not turning, he's stuck…" said the midwife.

"Oh, my God," said Anthony.

"Kate, I'm going to cut you. Hold on."

"What, what are you doing?" asked Anthony.

"Episiotomy, a cut, so you don't rip," said the midwife.

Kate cried out in pain. The doctor came back in.

"What's going on?"

"It's coming. It's definitely OP, and I'm worried about oxygen."

Kate was sobbing between cries of pain. Tears streamed down Anthony's face. His jaw was clamped tight as he tried not to make a sound.

"Okay, that's it. Prep her for theatre. I'm not taking any chances," the doctor said.

***

"He's beautiful," said Kate.

"I can't believe he's actually here," said Anthony.

"I thought this little fella was never coming."

"Maybe he knew the kind of world he was coming into."

"No, none of that now, please. Can't we just enjoy it?"

"Yeah, of course, we can, and I meant it, you know, every word of it. I'm going to look after you two."

"Does that mean what I think it means?" asked Kate.

"Yes, it does—a proper job with proper money. We'll be alright. I won't let you down."

"You know, don't you?" asked Kate.

"Know what?"

"That I love you. We love you."

***

"All very touching."

"Come on, even you must admit that's amazing. That's your son as well as mine. However, you think I might have let you down. Did you see him? He's your real future."

"Full of promises as usual, 'I'm going to look after

you.'"

"I meant it."

"Until?"

"Until what?"

"Well, something must have happened. You're divorced. Something new come along, did it? Get bored of the old commitments? Time to make new promises to new people?"

"It wasn't like that. We tried really hard. I was with Kate for over ten years. It was not easy to leave. We just grew apart. If you ask me, then, no, I am not proud of it. We used to have a saying for it, 'The Great Rift,' you know, like the valley. We didn't know how or when, but we found ourselves at either side of it with no way across. Her with the kids, me on the road all day. In the end, it was easier to be apart than to fight to keep it going."

"You see, that's what I'm on about. It's what happens when you let go of your principles. Easy come easy go. Pretty soon, anything is possible. It's like a slippery slope, and you have been sliding down it for too long."

"That's not fair."

"Fare is what you pay the bus conductor. Am I wearing a uniform?"

"This is ridiculous. The world has changed; people move on. For Christ's sake, Nelson Mandela was president of South Africa. We had a Labour government for over ten years. Things are different now. Sinn Fein is in the Northern Ireland government. It's a new world out there."

"Oh, right, so you're telling me in your world, the wars in Afghanistan and Iraq didn't happen? That poverty has been eradicated? That unemployment and food banks don't exist? That social opportunity doesn't depend on social class?"

"Well, not quite, no. In fact, if anything, things are getting worse. We're in the middle of a bloody depression."

"So, this is the ideal time to fight."

"Things are different now. Nobody's in unions anymore. The issues have changed. It's all about the environment and identity. Nobody talks about class. It's a different world out there."

"It feels different because you have cut yourself off from it. If you're not already, you will soon be on the other side. Worried about your job and your mortgage, you'll be blaming foreigners and lazy people. I don't want to become that."

"Okay, look, I know I am not what you expected to be or wanted, but you've got to try and see it from my point of view. You don't understand the pressure I'm under. I have to pay the maintenance for the kids. I'm still paying half the mortgage, her car, and mine. It's a nightmare."

"It's a nightmare, alright, but mine, not yours. The memories are coming back, thick and fast now, aren't they? Dipping into your memory is like lowering myself into a cesspit. Prostituting yourself, as a travelling sweets salesman, selling sugar-filled rubbish. Do you know how demeaning that is? Do you want to see your latest glory, do you? The very day they wheeled you here."

***

"Hey, Bartok," Anthony called out as he entered the

petrol station retail area.

"Tony, I wasn't expecting you. I was going to fax my order in."

"Yeah, I know, mate, but we've got this new product I didn't want you to miss out on. It's going to be really big. Lots of advertising around it. It's going to make a big splash."

"Splash like water? Drink."

"No, it's a bar. Splash means like a big launch. Hold on a second." Anthony's phone rang. He pulled it from his jacket. "It's the boss. I've got to take it," he said.

"No problem."

Tony retreated to the back of the store.

"Hi, this is Julie. Mr Schofield can't see you this afternoon. Something has come up. He's asked me to reschedule. When are you free?"

"I'm just ten minutes away now if it's good for him," Anthony said.

"Hold on, I'll check…Yeah, all good. Ten minutes it is, then. See you soon. Bye."

Tony put the phone away.

"Here, Bartok, I've got to run, mate. Here, have these free samples." He put six of the new chocolate bars on the counter. "I'll be back, got to go see my boss. Enjoy."

He waved as he left the shop.

***

"How's it going out there?"

"Good, yeah, sales up every month for the last year," said Anthony.

"That's the spirit. No matter how bad things get, people always need chocolate," said Mr Scofield.

"Need it, even more, the way the world is going."

"That's exactly right. That's why you're here, Tony, that kind of vision, optimism."

"Okay, I'm all ears," said Anthony.

"The thing is, you know, there have been rumours of a shakeup, re-engineering of the company as they like to call it."

"Yeah," said Anthony.

Mr Schofield leaned forward, elbows on his desk. "This shakeup means there might be an area manager's position, for the right person, of course."

"Isn't that Andy Parson's role?" Tony asked.

"Yeah, it was. I mean is. But between you and me, he has some family problems, had a bit of time off. Lost focus as it were. God knows I sympathise—there's nothing worse than a sick child. But we have to be realistic. The world doesn't stop turning, our competitors don't slow down, we have to keep up the pace, or we lose the race. Isn't that right?"

"Yeah, I guess so."

"This re-engineering means we can move Andy aside as part of the larger reorganisation, if you know what I mean. There could well be an opportunity for somebody willing to grasp the nettle. Is that you, Anthony?"

"Errh, I'm not sure," he replied.

"Of course, it would mean a significant regrading, with all the benefits, higher salary, car. We would need someone who...how can I put it...someone with a decisive bent, not afraid to shake things up a little. Andy might not be the only casualty. Do you know what I mean?"

"Yeah, I think so."

"That sounds great." Mr Schofield came out from behind his desk. "There will be a formal process, of course, but it's wise in situations like this to be ahead of the game. Let's just say we have an understanding, agreed?"

"Agreed."

***

"I'm back, mate. Did you try it?" Anthony said.

"Yeah, nice. Karoly, what did you think?" Bartok said.

Karoly, on the next cash register, gave him the thumbs up. "Good stuff."

"There you go, then. I tell you what, you order a case, 12 boxes, and I will throw in a free box. It uses up all my samples, but you guys are my favourite customers."

"How many in a box?" asked Bartok.

"Twenty-four mate, that's twenty-four free Global bars. You can sell them, eat them, throw a party if you like. You can do what you want with them."

A customer at the next till started arguing with Karoly. "I gave you a twenty, mate."

Bartok and Anthony turned as the customer reached across to grab Karoly.

"No, ten-pound. I have it here, ten, not twenty."

"Don't try this shit with me. You might do that in your own country, but you can't come here robbing me," the customer shouted. He reached across again to try and grab Karoly.

Bartok moved out from behind his register and approached the customer. "I'm the manager, sir. Let me take your number. I'll check the till later and call you. Sorry if it's a mistake. I call you later, give you ten pound."

"Are you calling me a liar? I want my money now," he demanded.

"No, sir. No liar. Not now, sorry, sir. It's rules. I call you later."

"You robbing bast—."

He grabbed the front of Bartok's shirt and pulled him toward the exit. "Come on outside…you're not robbing me and getting away with it."

He pulled Bartok toward the door. "We'll sort this out man to man."

He dragged Bartok outside.

***

"I've seen enough, heard enough. I'm not waiting around for twenty years to turn into everything I despise. When I think about the hopes, I had…"

"Can't you see? That's all they were. Your hopes were dreams and fantasies. That you would be some kind of people's hero, come to the rescue, save the world. But it's not like that. It doesn't work like that. What you saw is not pretty, but it's reality. I have to scheme and dodge, keep my head down, and my mouth shut. Why? It's called survival."

"What's the point of that kind of existence?"

"Because right now, it's the only one I've got."

"Yes, the only one you have got. But that's down to you.

You made this mess."

"How do you work that out? Am I responsible for history? Did I make the miners lose, or the Sandinistas in Nicaragua? Is it my fault Blair invaded Iraq? Tell me, how can I be blamed for these things?"

"You're not solely to blame, but what really hurts is that you don't even care. You used to be a citizen of the world. Now you are a citizen of nowhere. You are invisible. You might as well not exist."

"You can't do this. My kids need me."

"No, you need them…as an excuse for living. They stopped needing you when you deserted them. And do you know what? If you leave, you're better off out of the picture completely. Give them a chance to recover."

"But they are your kids. You'd see them without a father?"

"I'd see them without a disaster of a father, spending half their adult lives getting over feelings of guilt from your desertion. So, yes, I would, and if you loved them, really loved them as you claim, you'd see I was right."

"No, no, wait," said Anthony.

"No more waiting, no more excuses. The only power I have left is to take you with me. We'll both disappear forever. So say goodbye to your job, your property, and your dysfunctional family."

"You said you were a citizen of the world, right?"

"Yes. Of, but not belonging to any country," Tony clarified.

"Well, I am a citizen of time. We both are. That's why

things have happened the way they have."

"What are you saying?"

"What I'm saying is that people can't live independently of the times in which they are born."

"So?"

"So, what I'm saying is 'the times maketh the man.' I couldn't be who you were because of what happened to the miners. The force of my will alone, or your will, couldn't change what was happening around us."

"This sounds like an excuse."

"Think about it…great people have great stages on which to appear. Mandela might have just been a kindly old man without the upsurge of South Africans for freedom. Napoleon would probably have died a lowly lieutenant without the French Revolution."

"But individuals have an impact on the world around them."

"Of course, they do, but what is there to say they will see that impact in their own lifetime? Everything is a product of historical struggles, right?"

"Yeah."

"Can't you see? I can't live outside my time, just like you couldn't live outside yours. Alexander the Great would have been nothing without Phillip of Macedon, his father. Trotsky, Castro, all of them were dependent on the era they lived through, and so are we. Being a citizen of time means we can't prescribe when or how change will happen. All we can do is contribute to it."

"But that's my point—you're not contributing

anything."

"When I said my kids were the future, I meant it. They are the ones like our grandparents, who will see world-changing events in the times and struggles to come. And you will be part of them. You will have made your contribution."

"From what I've seen, a negative contribution."

"Don't sell yourself short."

"What do you mean?"

"I know now how I got here."

"I have seen your last day, watched you crawling to your boss. 'Yes, Sir,' 'No, Sir.' You want me to connive to get rid of a colleague? Then sit back and watch others lose their jobs? So I can climb the next rung on the ladder? Oh, while all that is going on, I will just stand back and watch a racist attack? If that is all, you have to offer? Then you had better face up to it. It's over. Finished."

"I said, don't sell yourself short. Do you really think everything I once was is finished? With no trace? How could you ever believe the world could be a better place if your view of yourself was so negative? In your world, can we not grow? Are we not allowed to make mistakes and learn from them? If you take me now, you will be denying the future you claim to want. You will be denying our ability to guide and influence my children through the struggles ahead. Worst of all, you really will be committing suicide. You're not dead, and if anything, I'm here because I was defending you, defending what I once stood for, my humanity. You said you can only see what I see, well look. This is why I am here. It's why we are both here."

***

Anthony rushed out of the shop. "Hey, leave him alone."

"You stay out of it. It's between me and this lying Polack."

"It's okay," said Bartok, his hands up defensively.

Anthony put himself between Bartok and the customer. "No, it's not okay."

He pulled a ten-pound note out of his pocket. "Here's your lousy tenner, now go on piss off, you racist shit."

The customer pushed, Anthony fell in front of an oncoming car. A screech of brakes, but too late, the impact.

***

"Mum, I think he's waking up. His eyes are opening."

"Stay here. I'm going to get the doctor," said Kate.

"Was it because we were playing his old music, mum?"

"I don't know. Stay here. I'll be back in a minute."

"Dad, Dad. Can you hear me, Dad? Mum said, you liked this song. Did it help wake you, Dad?"

"Yes, it did, son."

The sound of the Clash singing, 'Washington Bullets' filled the hospital room.

The End

Author's Note

Thank you for reading this collection of short stories. They were written over a period of about ten years. My debut novel Under The Bridge, book 1 in The Liverpool Mysteries, was published by Northodox Press in 2021.

I have worked in many jobs, including engineering and car factories, and I also started a couple of businesses, some more successful than others. Whatever I was doing, I always eventually returned to writing.

I left All Hallows school in Speke, Liverpool, with no qualifications. I went to University when I was forty years old after my first unpublished novel was written. After university, I returned to the business I was in at the time.

What changed was that in 2019 while running a small language school. I gave one of the teachers a chapter from Under The Bridge. He liked it, and he kept asking for more. I finally had an enthusiastic audience. I finished that book, Under The Bridge, and soon after started on the second, The Morning After. What started as one book has now developed into a series of four novels, two and a half, written, and one more to go. I am still working as a teacher. I have a family and so work like anyone else to pay the bills. But I am getting closer to my goal of becoming a full-time writer.

I set my books in the working-class community of Liverpool because it is where I am from, and real life contains all the comedy, drama, and tragedy needed for a good story.

If you enjoyed these stories, I would really appreciate a review on Amazon; you will be helping me reach my goal. All you have to do is say why you liked it, just one or two sentences is more than enough and leave a star rating.

If you are in the UK
https://amzn.to/38qzvwo

If you are outside the UK
https://amzn.to/3iu60OR

What's Next

The Morning After

The morning after the Brexit vote in 2016, history professor Vinny's world is turned upside down. What starts as a minor traffic incident grows in importance as the truth behind it is revealed.

Part family saga, part historical novel, all political mystery/thriller, South Liverpool comes to life in this novel in a world of daily struggles.

A secret Vinny, Sammo, and Macca vowed to keep as kids shackle them emotionally to a life-changing day, involving the theft of a pocket watch and an old man's death.

2016, Sammo is found dead, but his death is questionable, and with it, the past steps into the present. In his quest to find out what happened, Vinny uncovers more than he wants to know. Will Vinny do what is right, accept who he is? Will he let go of the secret he holds and the truth he discovers about community, humanity, and solidarity?

This page-turner is a story of the life and times of a group of young friends and the nation to which they belong. Defining moments in 1981 and 2016 bookend this dramatic story of secrets and lies, death, and disaster, showing how we got to Brexit and beyond.

Stay in touch:
Jack.byrne.writer@gmail.com
For news and updates:
Facebook: Jack Byrne
Web: https://jackbyrne.home.blog/

Printed in Great Britain
by Amazon

38644524R00081